Drama High, volume 17
Sweet Dreams

by
L. Divine

Praise for *Drama High*

L. Divine listed as one of the "Great authors for Young Adults."
-JET Magazine

"...Attributes the success of Drama High to its fast pace and to the
commercial appeal of the
series' strong-willed heroine, Jayd Jackson."
—*Publisher's Weekly* **on the DRAMA HIGH** series

"Abundant, Juicy drama."
—*Kirkus Reviews* **on DRAMA HIGH: HOLIDAZE**

"The teen drama is center-court Compton, with enough plots and sub-
plots to fill a few episodes of any reality show."
—*Ebony* **magazine on DRAMA HIGH: COURTIN' JAYD**

"You'll definitely feel for Jayd Jackson, the bold sixteen-year-old
Compton, California, junior at the center of keep-it-real Drama High
stories."
—*Essence* **Magazine on DRAMA HIGH: JAYD'S LEGACY**

"Our teens love urban fiction, including L. Divine's Drama High series."
—*School Library Journal* **on the DRAMA HIGH** series

"This book will have you intrigued, and will keep you turning the pages.
L. Divine does it again and keeps you wanting to read more and more."
—*Written* **Magazine on DRAMA HIGH: COURTIN' JAYD**

"Edged with comedy...a provoking street-savvy plot line, Compton
native and Drama High author L. Divine writes a fascinating story
capturing the voice of young black America."
—*The Cincinnati Herald* **on the DRAMA HIGH** series

"Young love, non-stop drama and a taste of the supernatural, it is sure to
please."
—*THE RAWSISTAZ REVIEWERS* **on DRAMA HIGH: THE FIGHT**

"Through a healthy mix of book smarts, life experiences, and down-to-
earth flavor, L. Divine has crafted a well-nuanced coming of age tale for
African-American youth."
—*The Atlanta Voice* **on DRAMA HIGH: THE FIGHT**

Other titles in the *Drama High* Series

THE FIGHT

SECOND CHANCE

JAYD'S LEGACY

FRENEMIES

LADY J

COURTIN' JAYD

HUSTLIN'

KEEP IT MOVIN'

HOLIDAZE

CULTURE CLASH

COLD AS ICE

PUSHIN'

THE MELTDOWN

SO, SO HOOD

STREET SOLDIERS

NO MERCY

DEDICATION

This volume is dedicated to Richard "5th Street Dick" Fulton. During my tenure as a coffee girl at 5th Street Dick's I learned so much, met so many people, fell in love with my own writing, and rekindled my interest in Chess and Jazz music. It is also where I met people who would forever change my life. Working at 5h Street Dick's was the path less chosen, no doubt. Thank you, Richard, for choosing and trusting me with your care and your business during the last years of your life. It was the only job I've ever had where I was encouraged to write, to explore, to read, to think and to act differently. It was where I started my first set of locs. It is where I delivered my first poem to a truthful audience. It was also where I learned more about so many different ways of thought and artistic revolution. Lemeirt Park became home, until it was ultimately time for so many of us to go.

There are too many people to name who became family but each of you had a part in helping me create Divine Born Wisdom, a.k.a. L. Divine, a.k.a. Divine. General Black, I still have every picture you ever drew of me and you still get respect for giving them to me rather than selling them. To David, thank you for doing all of the shopping and making sure that we always had cups and coffee to sell if nothing else. To Irma for always keeping Richard's spirits up and his memory alive. To the countless musicians, artists, chess players and customers who made my 12-hour shifts fly by. I salute you, 5th Street Gladiators. We are indeed the shit.

Acknowledgements

A huge thank you to my devoted readers Shanice Marie Beckford, Juanesha Franklin, Iris Aaliyah Travis, Taylor Reese, Ameerah Holiday, and my other countless FB, Twitter, Instagram and just straight-up, all around #DramaHighSoldiers. It is you who fan the flames, keep the pages alive, and who I write for. Thank you for your continued faith in the series.

Thank you to Adisa Iwa, a timely soldier who hustles hard on the "other side" of Drama High. I have faith in your faith. To my Starbucks crew, Jennifer, Doug, and everyone else who keeps the good energy percolating. To Baba Kokayi/Kenneth and La'Trishia Stallings, thank you for your good energy as well. And to my mom, Dorothy Lynette, who constantly reminds me to continue to do what I love and leave the stress out of it.

And lastly, thank you to the Star Trek franchise, in particular Star Trek: The Next Generation. I know it's not a person but it might as well be one to me. Without this show I don't know if my imagination would have ever stretched as much as it did when I was a child, and the show continues to have a positive effect on my mind. Thank you for challenging my perceptions. Thank you for approaching sometimes outlandish and challenging subject matters that showed me how important it was to engage in critical thinking for my own work. Even though sometimes I feel like my writing is a blessing and a curse, I keep engaging in the written word because if I can have the same effect on even one of my readers that Star Trek has had on me, how can I stop?

THE CREW

Jayd
The voice of the series, Jayd Jackson is a sassy seventeen year old high school senior from Compton, California who comes from a long line of Louisiana conjure women. The only girl in her lineage born with brown eyes and a caul, her grandmother appropriately named her "Jayd", which is also the name her grandmother took on in her days as a Voodoo queen in New Orleans. She lived with her grandparents, four uncles and her cousin, Jay and visited her mother on the weekends until her junior year, when she moved in with her mother permanently. Jayd's in all AP classes at South Bay High—a.k.a. Drama High—as well as the president and founder of the African Student Union, an active member of the Drama Club, and she's also on the Speech and Debate team. Jayd has a tense relationship with her father, who she sees occasionally, and has never-ending drama in her life whether at school or at home.

Mama/Lynn Mae Williams
When Jayd gets in over her head, her grandmother, Mama, a.k.a Queen Jayd, is always there to help. A full-time conjure woman with a long list of both clients and haters, Mama also serves as Jayd's teacher, confidante and protector. With magical green eyes as well as many other tricks up her sleeve, Mama helps Jayd through the seemingly never-ending drama of teenage life.

Mom/Lynn Marie Williams
This sassy thirty-something year old would never be mistaken for a mother of a teenager. But Jayd's mom is definitely all that. And with her fierce green eyes, she keeps the men guessing. Able to talk to Jayd telepathically, Lynn Marie is always there when Jayd needs her, even when they're miles apart.

Esmeralda
Mama's nemesis and Jayd's nightmare, this next-door neighbor is anything but friendly. Esmeralda relocated to Compton from Louisiana around the same time that Mama did and has been a thorn in Mama's side ever since. She continuously causes trouble for Mama and Jayd, interfering with Jayd's school life through Misty, Mrs. Bennett and Jeremy's mom. Esmeralda has cold blue eyes with powers of their own, although not nearly as powerful as Mama's.

Misty
The original phrase "frenemies" was coined for this former best friend
of Jayd's. Misty has made it her mission to sabotage Jayd any way she
can. Now living with Esmeralda, she has the unique advantage of being
an original hater from the neighborhood and at school. As a godchild of
Mama's nemesis, Misty's own mystical powers have been growing
stronger, causing more problems for Jayd.

Emilio
Since transferring from Venezuela, Emilio's been on Jayd's last nerve.
Now a chosen godson of Esmeralda's and her new spiritual partner,
Hector, Emilio has teamed up with Misty and aims to make life very
difficult for Jayd.

Rah
Rah is Jayd's first love from junior high school who has come back into
her life when a mutual friend, Nigel, transfers from Rah's high school
(Westingle) to South Bay High. He knows everything about Jayd and has
always been her spiritual confidante. Rah lives in Los Angeles but, like
Jayd, grew up with his grandparents in Compton. He loves Jayd fiercely
but has a girlfriend who refuses to go away (Trish) and a baby-mama
(Sandy) that has it out for Jayd. Rah's a hustler by necessity and a music
producer by talent. He takes care of his younger brother, Kamal and
holds the house down while his dad is locked-up in Atlanta and his
mother strips at a local club.

KJ
KJ's the most popular basketball player on campus and also Jayd's ex-
boyfriend and Misty's on and off again boyfriend. Ever since he and
Jayd broke up because Jayd refused to have sex with him, he's made it
his personal mission to annoy her anyway that he can.

Nellie
One of Jayd's best friends, Nellie is the prissy-princess of the crew. She
used to date Chance, even if it's Nigel she's really feeling. Nellie made
history at South Bay High by becoming the first Black Homecoming
princess ever and has let the crown literally go to her head. Always one
foot in and one foot out of Jayd's crew, Nellie's obsession with being
part of the mean girl's crew may end her true friendships for good if
she's not careful.

Mickey

Mickey's the gangster girl of Jayd's small crew. She and Nellie are best friends but often at odds with one another, mostly because Nellie secretly wishes she could be more like Mickey. A true hood girl, Mickey loves being from Compton and her on again/off again man, G, is a true gangster, solidifying her love for her hood. She has a daughter, Nickey Shantae, and Jayd's the godmother of this spiritual baby. Mickey's ex-boyfriend, Nigel has taken on the responsibility of being the baby's father even though Mickey was pregnant with Nickey before they hooked up.

Jeremy

A first for Jayd, Jeremy is her white, half-Jewish on again/off again boyfriend who also happens to be the most popular at South Bay High. Rich, tall and extremely handsome, Jeremy's witty personality and good conversation keeps Jayd on her toes and gives Rah a run for his money—literally.

G/Mickey's Man

Rarely using his birth name, Mickey's original boyfriend is a troublemaker and hot on Mickey's trail. Always in and out of jail, Mickey's man is notorious in their hood for being a cold-hearted gangster and loves to be in control. He also has a thing for Jayd who can't stand to be anywhere near him.

Nigel

The star-quarterback at South Bay High, Nigel's a friend of Jayd's from junior high school and also Rah's best friend, making Jayd's world even smaller. Nigel's the son of a former NBA player who dumped his ex-girlfriend at Westingle (Tasha) to be with, Mickey. Jayd's caught up in the mix as both of their friends, but her loyalty lies with Nigel because she's known him longer and he's always had her back. He knows a little about her spiritual lineage, but not nearly as much as Rah.

Chase (a.k.a. Chance)

The rich, white hip-hop kid of the crew, Chase is Jayd's drama homie and Nellie's ex-boyfriend. The fact that he felt for Jayd when she first arrived at South Bay High creates unwarranted tension between Nellie and Jayd. Chase recently discovered he's adopted, and that his birth mother was half-black—a dream come true for Chase. He was also Jayd's first lover and always has her back no matter what.

Cameron
The new queen of the rich mean girl crew, this chick has it bad for Jeremy and will stop at nothing until Jayd's completely out of the picture. Armed with the money and power to make all of her wishes come true, mostly via Misty and Esmeralda, Cameron has major plans to cause Jayd's senior year to be more difficult than need be. But little does she know that Jayd has a few plans of her own and isn't going away that easily.

Keenan
This young brotha is the epitome of an intelligent, athletic, hardworking black man. A football player on scholarship at UCLA and Jayd's new coffee shop buddy, he's quickly winning Jayd over, much to the disliking of her mother and grandmother. Although she tries to avoid it, Jayd's attraction to Keenan is growing stronger and he doesn't seem to mind at all.

Bryan
The youngest of Mama's children and Jayd's favorite uncle, Bryan is a deejay by night and works at the local grocery store during the day. He's also an acquaintance of both Rah and KJ from playing ball around the neighborhood. Bryan often gives Jayd helpful advice about her problems with boys and hating girls. He always has her back, and out of all of her uncles gives her grandparents the least amount of trouble.

Jay
Jay is more like an older brother to Jayd than her cousin. He lives with Mama and Daddy, but his mother (Mama's youngest daughter, Anne) left him when he was a baby and never returned. Jay doesn't know his father and attended Compton High School before receiving his GED this past school year. He and Jayd often cook together and help Mama around the house.

Jayd's Journal

Although I didn't want to take the chance of waking Chase up out of his peaceful slumber again, I couldn't take the risk of losing what I just learned. According to Queen Califia, if I don't want my mom and Mama—or even her for that matter—taking a look at what I'm thinking, then I can remove one jade bracelet at a time while calling out the person's name that I want to block. That's some wickedly cool shit right there. If I'd only known about this neat little trick sooner I could have been using it all along.

Mama doesn't know it yet but after what I uncovered in Cameron's room, I'm no longer looking to her or Netta for advice on how to deal with Esmeralda and her evildoers once and for all. And the nerve of Jeremy defending that heffa after she resorted to using voodoo dolls to fix me and my grandmother to do her will. As if I'd let that shit ride into the sunset just so I could be his chick again on the low. Please! As of now Cameron and her spiritual ill-advisor are mine for the taking, Jeremy be damned. All I care about is taking down my enemies one dream at a time and Esmeralda's first on my list. As the queen bee, when I take her down hopefully her drones will become completely incapacitated and make the rest of my job that much easier.

PROLOGUE

"Jayd, give me your hand," Rah says, guiding me down a steep cliff leading toward the ocean. "You know it's just supposed to be you and me. You've always known that in your heart."

"But it's not, Rah. That's the point," I say, doing my best to ignore the heat growing in my belly. "It's you, me, and several other people. It'll never just be the two of us."

"It's just the two of us right now," Rah says. He stops a few feet away from the water and sets down his bag. "Here, we can lock out the whole world and focus on the love that only you and I can make."

Rah takes me in his arms and holds me tight. I am completely swept up in the fantasy that he's created. He lifts my chin and positions my lips up to meet his. I don't hold back, equally responding to every bite and nibble that he takes.

"Rah, I can't," I say, thinking about the fact that I've already been down this road last night with Chase. "I'm already seeing someone else, and you've got your harem to deal with."

"Not in here we don't. In this world, it's just you and me. And as far as I'm concerned we are both going to be each other's first tonight."

Rah opens the bag and takes out a bamboo mat. He lays me down and then allows me to take control of the situation. Choosing to go with the

flow, I move from underneath him and pin him down, which causes a wide
smile to spread across his face.

"No more talking," I say. I look out toward the ocean and then back
down at Rah. "If we say the wrong thing it might cause us to both wake up,
and I'm not ready for that to happen just yet."

"It's your world, Queen. I'm just glad that you chose to share it with
me."

"Rah," I passionately moan. The shear force of our virtual
lovemaking pulls me out of my sleep. I shake myself fully awake,
grateful that Chase is already out of bed. What the hell? I have to be
more careful with my fantasies, but how can I control my emotions when
they're so clearly out of my control?

"Jayd, breakfast is ready," Mrs. Carmichael calls from downstairs.

"Thank you, Mrs. Carmichael. I'll be down in a second."

"Jayd, please. Stop being so formal. Call me Lindsay. We're
practically family now." At least one of us is sure about that.

I roll out of bed and walk into the adjoining bathroom to freshen
up. A girl can definitely get used to the beach life. Staying in Palos
Verdes has been nothing short of a dream, with fresh fruit and pastries

every morning for a picture-perfect breakfast on the balcony overlooking the beach.

I still don't know about taking Chase's mother up on her offer to stay here until my mom's ride is back in commission, but I must say that the thought is more and more tempting by the moment. I'd miss being at home, of course, but as much as I move around home is truly relative.

"If there's nothing to hide then spill it."
-Chase
Drama High, volume 12: Pushin'

~ 1 ~

NO PLACE LIKE HOME

After last week's dramatic ending with me finally ratting out Cameron and Laura in front of their mothers and Principal Shepherd for the lying wenches that they are, I have to say I'm happy that the school morning has been peaceful. I was expecting a bit of a backlash but so far so good.

I still haven't finished my midterm paper for English and need to find time to work on it. Mrs. Bennett's been unusually laid back lately. I don't know what she's up to, but I'm sure this is just the quiet before the storm.

"Jayd, what's up, chica?" Maggie asks, joining me and the rest of the students moving between class periods. We have a special lunch assembly and the shorter class periods have created more rushing about than usual.

"Nothing much, honey," I say, returning the love. "Are you ready for homecoming?"

"I was born ready, Miss Lady. But what I want to talk about is you meeting mi familia," Maggie says.

I'm still in a tailspin over that one. The fact that Chase's weed partners are Maggie's relatives, and at the same time Esmeralda's enemies, is still such wonderful coincidence that it must've been meant to be.

"Yeah, Javier and Mauricio seem real cool, Maggie. And I think they're just the ones to help me stop Esmeralda for good."

"Oh, mami. I know they are. Esmeralda has been in a thorn in mi Tia Beatrice's ass for many years. And don't get me started on Hector," Maggie says, as exasperated with Emilio's godfather as I am. "He's always been a culito."

"I guess the little asshole doesn't fall too far from the tree," I say, catching the back of Emilio's head as he enters the main hall through the center doors.

"No it does not," Maggie says, rolling her blue-mascaraed eyes at Emilio and his girlfriend, Misty, who greets him at his locker with a kiss. "Hopefully, stopping Esmeralda will also slow Misty's trifling ass down. I'd like just one year without her drama ruining it."

"Now you know there will always be drama at South Bay High no matter where it comes from," I say, smiling. They don't call this Drama High for nothing.

As if on cue, Nellie, Laura and Reid walk into the main hall behind a few other ASB members. They're being very aggressive in their campaign to win votes for Nellie's homecoming queen nomination but I'm not worried about it. Along with the African Student Union, El Barrio, the Hispanic clique on campus, will secure enough votes to make sure that Maggie takes home the crown and makes history as the first Latina Homecoming Queen ever in the history of South Bay High.

"Don't forget to sign up for your senior packages this week," Kendra, one of the newest ASB members says in the busy hall. She's posting large fluorescent fliers with all of the information on them to make sure that the students spend as much of their parents' money on immortalizing their last year of high school as possible. They even have payment plans that include every single activity from now through prom including graduation. I can't even afford my cap and gown let alone a ring or all for the other accouterments that literally have senior written all over them.

"Remember to vote for ASB's already royal nominee, Nellie, for homecoming queen," Laura says, passing more fancy fliers to Kendra who promptly adds them to the bulletin board. "As your princess last year, Nellie's the only natural choice."

"Exactly," Nellie says, tossing her fresh weave over her left shoulder where I notice what looks like a fading bruise, compliments of her boyfriend, David, no doubt.

"Give it a rest, Laura," Maggie says in their direction. "Get ready to bow down, bitches. I'm the only one who's going to be crowned queen this year."

"You're not Beyoncé and I'm certainly not your bitch," Nellie says, stepping up to Maggie who doesn't back down.

Maggie's shorter than me and by all accounts considered a quiet girl. But it's the quiet ones that you usually have to worry about.

"You're not my bitch yet but you will be by next Friday. Make sure you wear waterproof mascara, princesa. We wouldn't want you streaking those pretty cheeks with tears, okay? No crying allowed in my homecoming court pictures." Maggie laughs at a flustered Nellie. I don't think I've ever seen Maggie so competitive before, and I like it.

"If only the character qualifications of all nominees were thoroughly vetted, we'd be able to maintain a certain level of class for school-wide events," Reid says, defending his organization's choice. I don't think that he gives a shit about Nellie. She's just an end to his means: total campus domination.

"I completely agree," I say, defending my organization's choice as well. "When are ASB elections again? I think we should throw our hat in the ring for president this year and add that exact concern to our platform. Maybe things would actually change for the better around here."

Most of the students ignore the scene we're causing but a few hang on to see if any blows will be thrown before third period.

"You'd definitely get my vote, Miss Jackson," Chase says, stepping into the crowded hall with Nigel in tow.

"Why thank you, Mr. Carmichael," I say, smiling at my friend with many benefits. We both agreed that it's best to keep our temporary living arrangements and changed relationship status on the low for now, maybe forever. We have enough to deal with without allowing our friends' opinions to influence our decision.

"You all should really know when to quit," Laura says, seething. "But we'll settle for your humiliation during half-time at next week's game."

"Yeah, whatever," Chase says, putting his arm around my shoulders. "Maggie's got this election in the bag."

Nellie's eyes dart from Chase's eyes down to mine full of jealousy. She's always been envious of our friendship, which is a large part of why they broke up in the first place. If her once ludicrous suspicions were finally confirmed she'd have a conniption fit and then some. Nellie had it made in the shade with Chase on her arm last year, and so did Alia for that matter. When chicks try to control a dude it's the quickest way to get him to leave. The same goes for girls, at least this one. I hate it when a dude gets too clingy.

"Aren't you confused, Chase?" Reid asks. "What happened to your loyalty for the Drama Club's nominee, or has your newfound blackness clouded your sense of judgment?"

Laura and Nellie chuckle at Reid's little joke, if he can even call it that.

"Careful Reid," Chase says, letting go of me to step to Reid properly. "I have no problem showing you exactly where my loyalties lie."

"Again, class and character are completely underrated at our beloved school. What a shame." Reid and his arm candy exit the hall and leave their stench behind like a stale fart.

"Adios mio, they could work Jesus' nerves," Maggie says, crossing her chest with her fingers before kissing them.

"Agreed, but don't let them get to you," I say, reassuring our girl. "They live for rattling folks' nerves."

"Yeah, Maggie," Chase says, stepping in between me and Maggie. "Don't worry about them. You better than anyone should know that we always have a few tricks up our sleeves. Ain't that right, Madame President?" He wraps an arm across each of our shoulders and escorts us into the quad before we go our separate ways.

I need to get a move on most of all. No matter how good a mood she's been in lately, Mrs. Bennett waits for no one, especially not her least favorite student.

"Of course," I say, deserting them as we reach the Language Hall. "See y'all at the assembly."

"I'll save you a seat," Chase says, winking at me.

To be keeping us a secret he sure is getting a bit too friendly at school. I'll have to talk to him about that later. Right now I need to make it through this class and the next one without incident.

Thank goodness for the expedited school day. When classes are shorter it makes the day go by so much faster. I am going to miss high school periods when I'm in college. If nothing else they sure do help the day move along. Instead of being a typical assembly, it ended up turning into an announcement of sorts for the top athletes and which schools are heavily recruiting the seniors. KJ and Nigel are most likely going to either UCLA or USC, and Emilio's being recruited by Long Beach State for baseball. I never even knew that he was an athlete, but that's not surprising. I'm not a fan of Emilio's or baseball.

By the time the bus dropped me off in front of Dr. Whitmore's office my mom was ready to roll. Netta had already packed up Mama's things that morning but had to go back to work for the rest of the day. Her sisters can only be trusted to handle so much during Mama's absence. I've spent the last hour unpacking Mama's suitcases from Dr. Whitmore's place and putting everything back into her closet and dresser drawers just like she likes them. My mom helped Mama get re-acclimated to the spirit room in the back house, which Mama was grateful is just how she left it due in large part to me.

Mama's homecoming was less than eventful to all of her sons except for my Uncle Bryan who's been staying with his girlfriend lately. They didn't even notice how weak she looked, or how she stared at every single thing she saw when she walked slowly from the front door, through the living room, into the hallway, and finally into the bedroom we once shared. Everything seems so new to her, as if the past couple of weeks that she's been under quarantine at Dr. Whitmore's was a lifetime, and the home she once knew is now foreign.

"Jayd, where are my house shoes?" Mama asks, visually searching for them without moving from her bed.

"Right here, Mama," I say, lifting the bedspread on her twin bed and revealing the soft, pink slippers. I've had the pleasure of fetching her many pairs of house shoes for as long as I can remember.

"Oh, thank you, baby. I guess I'd better get started on dinner," Mama says, slipping into her shoes. "Your grandfather should be coming in from church any moment now."

"Say what?" my mom says, looking at her mother quizzically. "When's the last time you had dinner ready and waiting for Daddy to come home?"

My mom and I both look at each other and then back at Mama, completely confused.

"Lynn Marie, you're so silly sometimes. I swear I don't know where you get it from," Mama says, making her way to the kitchen.

We dutifully follow.

"Silly? Mama, what's gotten in to you?" my mom asks. "The last thing I'd expect for you to do when you got home is to cook for the same husband you vowed never to serve again."

"Hush your mouth talking about my husband like that," Mama

says, smacking her oldest child on the hand like she's five-years old.

I'm just as shocked, but I'll let my mom take the heat for the admonishment.

"You better take notes, young lady. This is how you keep your man happy and at home. Well, one of the ways," Mama says, winking at my mom who's completely mortified. "You're going to be a wife soon. So seriously, you should write some of this wisdom down while you can."

"Mama, are you feeling okay?" I ask, placing the back of my left hand on her forehead. "Maybe we should take you back to Dr. Whitmore's."

"Yeah, I agree. Mama, where are the herbs he gave you to take? We can't miss any doses," my mom says, equally concerned.

"Jayd, I'm fine, and no I don't need to see the good doctor," Mama says. She reaches into the cabinet to the left of the sink and pulls out the ingredients for her infamous cornbread.

I know something strange is going on, but I wouldn't mind a piece of her cornbread before I dig deeper into her suspicious behavior.

"I can't believe it. All my girls in one place," Daddy says, stepping into the kitchen through the back door.

Lexi, Mama's dog, follows him inside and takes her customary place underneath the table. She more than anyone is glad that Mama's home. Whatever her master goes through Lexi also feels.

"Hey Daddy," my mom says, kissing my grandfather. "How's the Lord's work?"

"Tough, as usual," Daddy says, kissing my forehead. "But it wouldn't be rewarding if it was easy." He then walks over to my grandmother to properly greet her.

"Just like any good marriage," Mama says, accepting Daddy's intimate kiss.

My mom and I look at each other awkwardly, both too shocked to speak out loud. Luckily for us we don't have to.

"I don't remember the last time my parents kissed," my mom says into my thoughts. *"What the hell is going on?"*

"I don't know, but whatever it is has got them acting like teenagers and I don't like it one bit," I think back. If I didn't know better I'd say that they were under some sort of love spell, but why? And cast by whom? I'm pretty sure that Esmeralda's the last person who would put a love spell on my grandparents—straight hate is more her style.

"Jayd, take out the rest of the ingredients for me and get started chopping the vegetables for beef stew."

"My favorite," Daddy says, kissing his wife's nose. "You haven't made that in years, Lynn Mae."

"I know. I'd say it's been too long since I pleased my man, wouldn't you?" Mama rubs her nose against Daddy's.

This is borderline abuse to my young eyes.

"Okay, there's a child in the room you two," my mom says, shaking her head, but nothing will erase the picture from our memories.

"She's right, Pastor James," Mama says, taking him by the hand. "You girls can handle getting dinner started. I'll be back." Mama leads Daddy toward her bedroom—the same room he was formally forbidden from entering years ago once Mama found out about all of his church girlfriends.

"Jayd, what the hell was that?" my mom whispers. "Seriously. That was weird, even for this family."

"I know, mom." I take an onion and a few garlic cloves from the basket on the table and do as I'm told. Even Lexi looks baffled by her owner's behavior. "But whatever it is seems to make Mama happy, and that's what she needs and deserves now more than anything, so I say we let it go for now."

"If you say so," my mom says, heading for the back door. I can tell she's ready to get back to her own man and her side of town. It's rare for my mom to stay in Compton any longer than necessary. "Are you staying the night here or coming back to Inglewood? I don't want you riding the bus too late."

"I'm actually going to stay over Chase's house tonight, and probably for a few nights until your car is back in commission," I say, chopping away. I guess my mom's not going to help at all.

"Is that so?" my mom says, smiling. "As long as it's okay with his mom and you're being careful, if you know what I mean."

"Mom, it's not like that," I say, feeling my cheeks heat up.

"Yeah, okay," my mom says, smacking my backside. "I was seventeen before, you know. You can't fool me, little girl. Just make sure you heed my warning. I'm too young to be a grandmother, you heard?"

"Good night, mom," I say, kissing her on the cheek.

"Good night, baby. And keep an eye on your grandmother."

Chase already told me to text him when I'm ready to leave. It feels weird but I am enjoying the royal treatment he gives. As long as I can keep my dreams somewhat in check so that Chase doesn't witness an unfortunate psychic love making session between me and Rah, I think we could make this new friendship with benefits work. I admit that it's a bit strange on so many levels but it also feels quite natural to go home with Chase, and his mom who's more than okay with it. They've always been like family to me and they are the only people I know who don't make me feel awkward in my own skin.

~ 2 ~

AWKWARD BLACK GIRL

It's the middle of the week and I still haven't been able to figure out what's up with my grandparents' rekindled mutual infatuation. My cousin Jay called me yesterday after he caught them kissing passionately in the hallway. They couldn't even make it to the bedroom three feet away. All I could say to him was that absence makes the heart grow fonder, and with Mama being "away" for a few weeks Daddy must've realized how much he'd suffer if she ever left him for good.

Mama's been like a new woman in more ways than one since her peck on the head from Esmeralda's crow. My main priority at the moment is to find a way to kill the messenger and permanently disable the sender. From what Dr. Whitmore could tell, Mama's back in top shape. As a matter of fact, she's better than ever. Now that we have possession of all of our voodoo dolls we've been able to take full advantage of using them for our own good before placing them inside of our vessels for safe keeping. In my studies I've come across a couple of different incantations that have positive side effects outside of whatever they were originally used for, which I think explains Mama and Daddy.

I'll keep a close eye on my grandmother's behavior for any signs of evildoing, however I think their love is a positive side effect of dressing her doll properly and with pure love.

If only I could do the same thing with my friends. Mickey's working my very last nerve with her bull early this morning. I can already tell it's going to be a long-ass Wednesday. Life would be so much easier if I could just manipulate everyone to do what I want them to do. Too bad it would be considered unethical and a misuse of the powers in our lineage. From what I've read, the few times that it did happen the repercussions to the master manipulator were swift and brutal. Trust, if I thought it was a good idea, everyone would call me Geppeto by the time it was all said and done.

"I mean, you could've at least stuck around to get that shit on video so I can use it against Nigel and his mama for my case," Mickey says, continuing her rant against me disserting her at the college party last weekend. Keenan came to my rescue that night and not a moment to soon. I have yet to properly thank him for having my mom's car towed or for breakfast the next morning.

"Mickey, in case you forgot, I was dealing with my own drama that night. My mom's car getting broken into again was more urgent than you and Nigel going at each other's throats, as usual."

Chase dropped me off at the front of the school and then went to run a quick errand before the first bell. I don't know what kind of errand, but some things are best left in the dark.

"Whatever Jayd," Mickey says, opening one of the doors that lead into the front office. "All I know is that I could've used that shit against them in a court of law to get them off my ass for good."

"Really, Mickey? Do you think you yelling and screaming in public with your ex boyfriend and his mom, a pillar in the community, would bode well for you in court? And who says you're going to court anyway?"

"I say so," Mickey says, becoming even more indignant. "I'll be damned if he thinks that I can be bullied into giving him what he wants, I don't give a shit who his mama and daddy are."

The last thing I need is for this broad to cause a scene near the Principal's office. Principal Shepherd and me have a clear understanding: he doesn't want to see me in his office for the rest of the school year, and I don't want to be in there ever again.

"Mickey, I think you need to think this through," I say, lowering my voice as a subtle hint that she should also lower hers. "Have you even consulted an attorney about your rights? I can ask Mrs. Carmichael if she can help you out. Maybe you should also consider talking to Mrs.

Esop. There's got to be another way for you and Nigel to resolve this before it gets any uglier."

"What the hell are you talking about, Jayd? They came after me, not the other way around." I guess she didn't get my hint because her voice has gone in the opposite direction.

"Really, Mickey? Because I distinctly remember you trying to get in good with Nigel's mom before you decided that it wasn't to your benefit anymore," I say, reminding her that around this time last year she sunk her claws deep into Nigel as soon as he stepped foot on this campus. Once she was done playing house, she threw him aside to get back with her man when he was released from jail, also taking her baby, my goddaughter, with her to complete their dysfunctional family picture.

"I'm not trying to kiss Nigel's ass or his mama's ass to keep my own damn daughter, Jayd. No, I'm not doing it! Forget them, and forget Chase's mama, too. I'm not asking for her advice; me and G got this."

"You and G," I say, shaking my head. "Mickey, all you care about is being taking care of no matter who your delusional version of Prince Charming may be. You need to get over your Cinderella tendencies and think about what's in the best interest of your daughter. Have you

33

even thought about your college applications? It will look good to the judge if you're thinking about your future."

"I don't have Cinderella tendencies, Jayd," Mickey says, stopping near the double doors leading from the front office into the main hall where our lockers are located. "And I'm not applying to college because I'm not going. I have street dreams, Jayd, and I'm thinking about real shit, not some fantasy where we all go to college and pledge a sorority and all of that bull that Nigel's mom sold you."

"It's not bull," I say, feeling a bit exposed. Am I really that transparent? I never thought of myself as a sorority chick, but college has always been on my radar. "Mickey, I know college isn't for everyone but you haven't applied yourself this year, and that's not going to sit well with the judge. If Nigel's mom has her way she'll have the courts subpoena your school records and that's not a very good look for you, Mickey." She has enough absences, tardies, and other disciplinary actions on her record to speak volumes, and that's not including her lackadaisical grades.

"If Nigel's mom wants a fight she can bring it right to my front door," Mickey says, shifting her weight from one immaculately pedicured foot to the other. "She hasn't dealt with me or my family before, especially not G's side, and they don't play that bougie Lafayette Square bull."

"Mickey, haven't you learned anything from your interactions with Mrs. Esop?" I say, trying to conjure up the many embarasising encounters Mickey's already had thanks to Nigel's mom. "She's not going to back down and you know that she can be real nasty when she wants to be."

Mickey steps up to me as if I'm Mrs. Esop's personal messenger. "Bitches gone be bitches, Jayd. And I say let bitches be."

"Okay, Mickey," I say, stepping back. I don't mind standing up for myself when necessary but I'm not willing to get into a fight over Nigel's mom and his ex any day. "Have it your way."

"That's all I'm asking for." Mickey backs off and smiles as if she's won. She has no idea what she's up against.

Before we exit the office I notice Marcia, my new acquaintance, speaking to the school secretary. The conversation seems pretty intense.

"Hold up Mickey. Let me say hi to Marcia real quick," I say, walking backwards.

"Why do you need to talk to that girl? Are you going to recommend a make over?" Mickey says, turning her nose up.

"Mickey, chill." I lead the way over to where Marcia's standing. "She's nice."

"She seems nice enough but she looks like she's been sleeping outside," Mickey says.

Marcia's curly hair is wild and loose, her clothes aren't the neatest, and her cheeks look permanently sunburned. I'm not sure what nationality she is but her striking, green eyes can catch anyone off guard. She reminds me of all of the other women in my lineage with green eyes except for me, thus my name. If I didn't know any better, I'd say Marcia was a Williams' woman.

"Hey, Marcia. How's it going?"

"Hey, Jayd," Marcia says, looking at the class schedule in her hand. "Everything's okay, I guess. I just got my permanent schedule this morning but they made a mistake."

"What's the problem?" I don't know why but there's something about Marcia that makes me want to help her out.

Mickey impatiently waits by the exit. She's never been one for making new female friends. If it weren't for Nellie, Mickey and me probably wouldn't even know each other or even worse, we'd probably be enemies.

"I spell my name Marcia not Marsha, but its no big deal," Marcia says, disregarding the typo.

"Oh no, girl," I say, intervening like Misty did with me on my first day at South Bay High. Even if it's not officially her first day it's still not too late to show her the ropes. "If you don't correct it now they'll put it on all of your school records and you don't want that, especially not with us graduating in June. How's it going to look if they put the wrong name on your high school diploma?"

"I guess you do have a point there," Marcia says, forcing a smile. She hasn't had an easy first few weeks up here and I feel partially responsible since Nellie's uncalled for bullying of Marcia. At least I was there to check my wayward friend for following after the rich bitches instead of being cordial to the newbie.

I seize the paper from her and hand it back to the secretary. "Excuse me, ma'am," I say to the secretary. We've had more than one conversation and I can already tell that she's not feeling me this morning. "Her name was accidentally misspelled on her permanent schedule. We just want to make sure that it was an innocent typo and not on her school records."

She looks from Marcia to me as if to ask, "Why am I speaking up for this girl?" Instead of voicing her objection, she takes the paper and checks her computer screen. "Oh, you're right. I can fix that for you," the secretary says.

I wink at Marcia who smiles again in gratitude. "Trust me. My name is spelled with a 'y'. I constantly have to remind folks that it's not with an 'e' at the end."

"Here you are, young lady," the secretary says, handing Marcia the corrected schedule. "Enjoy your morning."

"See," I say, pointing to her corrected name. "Easy, breezy, beautiful, Cover Girl."

"Thank you," Marcia says, this time with a genuine smile across her face.

"No problem, Marcia."

"Seriously, you didn't have to do that, Jayd. I'm used to it," she says, following me toward the door where Mickey's posted up.

"It's no problem. Besides, like I said, people always spell my name wrong and I've never gotten used to it. You shouldn't either."

"Bout time," Mickey says, rolling her eyes as if she's in a rush to get the school day officially started. Even though we still have a few minutes before the first warning bell rings I'd bet ten dollars that Mickey will still arrive late to her class.

"And this is Mickey," I say, shaking my head at my rude friend. "I don't think you two have been properly introduced."

"Hi Mickey. I'm Marcia."

"What's up?" Mickey looks Marcia up and down like she's a peasant and Mickey's the freaking queen of Scotland. She's got her nerve.

We continue our trek toward the lockers in an awkward silence.

"Hey Jayd," Jeremy says, intercepting us in the middle of the large hall.

I haven't seen or spoken to him since the unfortunate doll incident at Cameron's house. I'm still too pissed at him to talk about it.

"Hey, Jeremy," Mickey says.

"Hi." It's too obvious that Marcia's enamored with my ex-boyfriend's good looks. Unlike most of the chicks up here—and some of the dudes—his charm no longer works on me. Along with being fine, Mickey thinks it was stupid of me to let him go because he's balling out of control.

"Hi Mickey and Marcia," Jeremy says, acknowledging them both.

I'm surprised that he remembers Marcia's name from the interrupted study session at Cameron's. Maybe they have classes in common I'm not yet aware of. Whatever. I could care less about who

Jeremy knows and doesn't know anymore. I've been dissed by him for the last time.

"Jayd, please," Jeremy says, blocking my way. "A moment."

"Why should I give you any of my time, Jeremy?" I say, making it clear to him and everyone else in the busy hall how over his apologies I am. "You've made it very apparent whose back you have and whose you don't have, even if I've always been there for you, more than you even know."

"Jayd, I know. I screwed up the other day, okay? I know I panicked at Cameron's house and I am so sorry about that shit," Jeremy says, sounding sincere. "Please, just hear me out. I know she was in the wrong and that you were just defending yourself."

"Well, I'm glad that you've been recently enlightened, Buddha, but I've always had my eyes opened regarding your girlfriend. Sorry that you're just waking up." I walk past him and toward my locker and catch up to Mickey and Marcia.

"Well, this is kind of uncomfortable," Marcia says into my ear. I would laugh but nothing's funny about me and Jeremy's drama—nothing at all.

Jeremy, still in hot pursuit, won't let me get too far ahead. "Jayd, look. I know this has been a complete mess to say the least. I want to correct every stupid decision that I've made. It's all been too much to handle and I know I've acted like a complete ass."

"You think?" I say, finally reaching my locker. Mickey's isn't too far ahead and I don't know where Marcia's locker is, but she's apparently not worried about it or she just doesn't want to miss the rest of the Jayd and Jeremy show.

"Okay, I deserve that," Jeremy says, putting his hands above his head like he's being arrested. "But Jayd, I figured out a way to get out of this mess once and for all."

I look past Jeremy to see Chase making his way toward us. Hopefully we can keep our feelings at bay in front of our crew. We had a discussion about how to proceed with keeping our budding relationship on the low, even if it is difficult when we can't help but smile at each other.

I refocus my attention on the issue at-hand. "I'm happy for you, Jeremy. But I've been more than patient with your situation. And quite frankly, at this point it would be too embarrassing if we got back together."

Jeremy looks completely shocked. I'm not certain, but I wouldn't be surprised if a girl has never spoken to him like this before. If it's the truth then I'm glad to be the first to set him straight. He can't continue walking around like he's the Czar of South Bay.

The warning bell rings and more students scramble into the already crowded hall. It's time to get moving whether we're ready to face the day or not, just like Jeremy's going to have to learn to face it that we're over—permanently this time. He and Rah are in my past, not matter what my dreams might say.

"Look Jayd, I know I don't deserve anymore of your time or another chance to make things right between us. But I can't let it go, not like this." Jeremy pulls a box out of his back pocket and hands it to me. "This would've been our one year anniversary if I hadn't screwed things up."

Damn, he's right. "I don't want anymore of your gifts," I say, rejecting the gesture. "I told you, I'm over it. All of it, Jeremy. Besides, I never wanted you for your money or what you could buy me." Him showering me with expensive gifts always made me feel uncomfortable.

Mickey catches my eye and gawks at me disapprovingly, as usual. When it comes to all things money Mickey is the world's leading material girl. She's always thought me foolish in that department—her and Nellie. But I can't be bought by anyone, and I won't accept gifts from those who hurt me no matter how heartfelt they may be.

"Don't you think I know that by now, Jayd? That's one of the reasons that I love you so much." He again tries to hand me the small brown box and again I refuse.

"I'm going be late to first period," I say. "See y'all at break."

"My people." Chase is just in time to escort me to class. "What's the good word?"

The look on my face tells Chase that this isn't a good time to joke.

"What's up, Chase?" Jeremy says, giving his friend dap. "Here, maybe she'll listen to you." Jeremy sighs deeply and hands Chase the gift. He looks down at me with red eyes. "Make sure she listens to number seven."

Jeremy walks back out of the hall the same way that he entered. I shake my head at the morning drama and again say goodbye to my friends. We each go our separate ways, all except for Chase.

"What did I miss?" Chase asks as we head toward the Language Hall.

"More shit, nothing new," I say, looping my left arm through his right. We've been tight since my first year at Drama High, so no one will suspect anything's up with us by showing our regular play brother and sister affection.

"Yeah, okay," he says, opening the box. "Your boy seemed pretty upset."

"It's not about Jeremy anymore," I say, still seething from the encounter.

"Well, I think Jeremy would disagree." Chase passes me the classic personalized iPod with "Lady J" inscribed on the back. "Listen to number seven," he says, repeating his boy's request.

"You're not funny, Chase." I take the gift from him and admire the old school device. These aren't easy to come by and they're not cheap.

"I'm not trying to be." Chase looks genuinely concerned and I can't help but feel bad that he's in the middle of this bull between his best friend and me. "In a minute," he says, heading toward his own class now that we've reached mine.

I claim my seat in the room with a minute to go until the late bell rings. I might as well listen to the chosen track just to see what it is. Creep by Radiohead. Of course.

I wish I could say that I hate Jeremy but I actually feel sorry for the way that our relationship ended. And in all honesty, I do miss our friendship. He's made some bad decisions and as Mama would say, he's not dangerous, just a stupid, stupid man. If I had my way we would've never broken up, but that was on him and his dumb ass habits. If he weren't high and drunk in the first place, then Cameron would've never been able to trap him in her sadistic fantasy.

Now granted, because of Misty's diabolic skills by way of Esmeralda, Cameron had a little more influence over him than she normally would have, but still, he should've been able to keep his own vices under control. No matter what kind of playlists he's put together, Jeremy and me are definitely a thing of the past. I'm not completely single, but I'm definitely noone's girlfriend anymore, and it's going to be like that for quite some time.

"I don't know how sweet I can be when someone's talking smack about my family."
-Jayd
Drama High, volume 16: No Mercy

~ 3 ~
# GRIS-GRIS

Since Mama and Daddy are apparently out on a date tonight, I decided to get to work on serving Esmeralda and Cameron a nice dish of revenge all on my own. I'll see Mama at Netta's shop tomorrow after school for our typical Friday duties, so I can give her the third degree in front of my godmother, who I'm sure will be just as interested in Mama's behavior as I am. Her and Daddy being affectionate isn't the real problem; I just want to make sure that it's not because of something Esmeralda's got a hand in.

It's been a long time since I worked on conjuring up a batch of tainted sweets by myself. It feels good to be in the spirit room on a solo mission. According to the instructions in the dream I had where Queen Califia showed me how to block my mom and grandmother from my thoughts, I carefully remove two of my jade bracelets from my arm and call their names while doing so. I place them in my Oshune vessel on Mama's shrine and get to work. The less intrusions I have the better.

With the help of Maman, I was able to snatch up a few strands of Esmeralda's hair to fix Cameron and Esmeralda's miniature counterparts. If she thinks that she's the only one who can fix voodoo dolls then she's sadly mistaken. I also snatched a bit of Cameron's hair out when I hit her to the ground last week, so I can make sure that they both get what they deserve and a little extra. Misty and Emilio will have to be handled a bit differently being that their souls are under Esmeralda's control. Until I can free them from their reptilian avatars there's not much I can do to them.

"Alright, Lexi. Let's see what these Cripple Crème Puffs can do," I say, pulling the delicate pastries out of the oven to allow them to cool.

Mama's dog looks at me skeptically, circles her tail, and reclaims another one of her customary spots by the door. She never judges me, or at least not that I can tell. It must be nice to chill all day. Lexi's been asleep the majority of the time we've been back here and it's been nearly three hours.

The goal is to spread the love to my main enemies by having Misty deliver them from her wack-ass godmother to Cameron. As long as they each take at least one bite these should work, and that's where the dolls will come into action. I don't want to hurt them physically, which is all the dolls can really accomplish. I want to disable them from the inside out to the point that every time they even think about doing something to the ones that I love they'll fall ill and forget what their

47

original mission was. And if they do happen to remember I've got the dolls for back up.

My phone rings with a text message. It's Keenan. I've been avoiding him for a minute now. I actually thought he gave up after the last message he sent went unanswered but apparently the brotha remains undeterred.

Jayd, what's up with you? Haven't heard from you in a minute. Still on for that study session? Kind of missing your energy.

Keenan can be sweet when he wants to be, but I honestly think that we're just too different to be anything more than acquaintances. I have to think carefully about how I want to respond. He has been invaluable as a friend in some ways, but at the end of the day I think his ego's going to be the end of whatever could have been between us.

"I think I'll join you for a few minutes until I can put the finishing touches on the dessert," I say to Lexi who's nearly asleep. It's been a long day with homecoming on Saturday and tests tomorrow in History, English and Spanish. Whoever thought it was a good idea to give tests on Fridays really should have thought about that more carefully. I'd like to end the week on an easy note but no such luck in my classes this semester.

I retrieve one of the bamboo mats leaning up against the wall and roll it out to lie down. A quick nap will do me some good. The sweet scent of powered sugar, flour and chocolate gananche creeps into my nose and help me to achieve a quick, restful slumber.

The vacant parking lot of the South Bay Galleria is brightly lit, but the car is parked in the one dark spot in the vast space. The jade stones in my pocket begin to glow the closer I get to the parked car. I recognize it as my mothers broke down vehicle.

"I've got the tools," a voice says from underneath the hood. "All I need is a little light and I can fix you right up."

"I don't need fixing," I say, finding the flashlight button on my phone and pressing it.

"You know what I mean." I can hear the smile in his voice, but who is my mysterious mechanic?

"Is this enough light?" I shine the bright ray toward his face but I still can't tell who it is.

"Yes, but it would help if you'd shine it where I'm working and not on me. You know what I look like, queen."

There's only one person who calls me that. Oh no, not another Rah dream.

"Jayd, did you hear me?" Rah asks, pushing himself out from under

the car. "I can't see what I'm doing unless you help a brotha out."

"My badd," I say. "I can't see where you're pointing."

"That's because you're standing up. I need you to lie down next to me. Don't worry. I won't bite, unless you want me to." He smiles at my obvious embarrassment and pushes himself back underneath the car.

I lie down on the towel next to him and shine the spotlight where he directs me to.

"Perfect," he says, manipulating the metal tools underneath the hood.

I really have to get in good with another person who has mechanical skills like Rah does or even learn to do some things myself. Chase and Jeremy like to work on cars but it's mostly esthetic, and Nigel can do about as much as Rah does but he doesn't like to get his hands dirty on the regular. Netta's son is okay, but I think Jeremiah's got too much on his plate as it is and besides, he's not the best at this type of work. I would never tell her that of course, but it's the truth.

"Thanks for handling this for me, Rah. I know you must be tired of taking care of my car."

"I could never get tired of taking care of any part of you, girl. You should know that by now."

Rah pushes out from under the car again, this time wiping his hands clean on his oil rag. He touches my cheek with the back of his hand, then moves down to my neck, shoulder, and then breast. Oh hell.

"Rah, I've really got to get going," I say, attempting to halt his advance. "It's getting late. I know Chase is probably worried by now."

"Chase is not my concern," Rah says, propping up on his side. "You are. And I must say, I think you're a little less than satisfied with that arrangement."

Before I can protest, he leans over and kisses my neck, my weak spot, and I allow him to distract my thoughts away from what I know I should be doing.

"Rah, the cameras," is all I can manage to say. The small, reflective black objects are in each of the corners in the outdoor parking structure. The last thing I need is me making out with Rah on the eleven o'clock news.

"It's just a dream, Jayd," Rah speaks into my ear. "Relax, I've got you covered." He pulls a condom out of his pocket and continues to explore my body with his soft lips.

"Rah, we shouldn't." Even if it is a dream I don't want to get caught up in another love affair with him. Wait a minute—how is he aware that I'm dreaming? Since when is he able to communicate with me in this state of mind?

51

"Since you dreamed it into existence," he answers. Now he's a mind reader too?

"You don't remember, but once upon a time you used your mom's sight on me, and saw right into my dream world while I was asleep. In that dream you and I could communicate just like this." Rah's moved down to my belly button, another one of my weak points.

"But that doesn't make any sense," I say, pushing him away. "Just because you could do it in a dream way back when doesn't mean you still can. You don't have any powers."

"I don't need any," Rah says, kissing my thighs. "You've got enough power for the both of us. It's your world, queen."

"So, essentially I'm in control of all of this right here," I say, emphasizing our physical situation with my hands, my only free body parts. Everything else on me is now covered by Rah.

"You've always been in control, Jayd. It's all about you. I'm here to make all of your dreams come true." Rah looks into my eyes and I notice that my reflection glows with a green hue. He's right; my mom's eyes are mine."

I suddenly no longer feel bad about being here with Rah. He's a beautiful man, his body is tight, and I've known him for years. He's also the first guy I can remember being strongly attracted to—and still am.

Rah resumes kissing me and I return his affection. I can't help it. I've always had passionate feelings for Rah, and in this world we're not hurting anyone. Why not rekindle our fire in the only safe way that we can?

The alarm goes off on my phone and saves me from myself, thank goodness. Well, that was interesting. I hate to admit it but I'm rather enjoying me and Rah's shared sweet dreams. I'm just not sure how long I can go without solidifying our sexual desires outside of the dream world. And also, as long as I'm sharing a bed with Chase I can't very well get caught up in an impassioned tryst with Rah. What if he hears me saying Rah's name, which I'm sure Rah would love in either world? The last thing I want is for Chase to feel like he as to deal with Jeremy and Rah vying for my attention.

No sense in worrying about that right now. I've been thinking about moving into one of the guest rooms for the remainder of my stay any way, but Chase seems very comfortable with our current arrangement, and I am used to being in his room, which is actually more like a second Master's suite. In lieu of my current predicament, I think I need to move when I get back to his house this evening. In the meantime, I'll put the finishing touches on tomorrow's special delivery one puff at a time.

Cleaning up is my least favorite part of baking, but at least it's a nice night. I place the plastic trash bag into the large garbage can next to the back gate, which is unfortunately adjacent to Esmeralda's back yard. My companion barks toward Esmeralda's house. I don't see or hear anything, but the way that the grey hairs are standing on the back of Lexi's neck tells me that there's definitely something there.

"What is it, girl?"

Lexi's frozen in a guttural growl.

"You should really warn your pet about the dangers of having a threatening stance," a familiar voice says, but I can't see who's speaking. "She could get in over her head, yet again." Esmeralda appears from behind the thick bushes that line her side of the fence with her favorite crow perched on her shoulder. She has no idea that her loyal servant betrayed her by helping me get the last ingredient I needed to work my charm on his master.

"Don't worry about my grandmother's dog, Esmeralda. You have enough furry friends to keep an eye on."

"Oh please, Jayd. I've always known how to keep my house in order, a skill your grandmother never mastered." Esmeralda places both hands on the boundary, displaying her angled acrylic nails pointed similar to the way Mickey likes hers done, but longer. "How is Lynn Mae these days, by the way? Is she back in her right mind yet?" Esmeralda's not slick at all.

"Again, not your concern, but I'll tell her that you asked." I take a step toward the spirit room and am stopped in my tracks by one of Esmeralda's legionnaires.

"Oh, don't be afraid, little girl. She won't attack until I tell her to."

The spider dangles from the tree branch above my head and blocks my path. Normally I'm not that afraid of spiders, but this is the largest black widow I've ever seen. Tonight is not the night for a sister to get bit.

"What do you want, Esmeralda?" I ask, tired of her little game. She won't be able to play like this anymore once I get to her tomorrow.

I'll have to be up extra early to catch one of her favorite neighborhood clients, Ms. Shreeva, walking up the block to greet her as she does nearly every morning. I never had much to say to her and won't tomorrow morning, either. All I need from her is to make eye contact and she'll be willing to deliver the laced treats right to their intended target.

"What do I want? What do I want, little Jayd?" Esmeralda repeats, almost laughing. "I want what any girl would. I want you and your grandmother to stay out of my business, and I'll stay out of yours. Agreed?"

"Nobody cares about your business, Esmeralda. It seems you're the one who keeps meddling where you shouldn't."

If she's knows what I know about her manipulating the drug dealers around here with her doll collection, including Mickey's man, then I know she's out for my blood, but what else is new? This bitch has been after my family since before my mother was born and the only way she'll back off is by force, which I intend to use whole-heartedly. The Crème Puffs are just the beginning of my attack strategy.

"Oh, Jayd. What's going on inside of that pretty little head of yours? Let's take a look, shall we?"

The spider begins to rapidly descend down her silken string toward the top of my head. I back up and look at Esmeralda who's covering her cold blue eyes with shades; I guess she doesn't want to take another chance at me getting inside of her head. Too bad she couldn't find a pair to fit her bird.

I lock onto the beady black eyes of her companion and focus intently on what I want it to do. *"Eat the spider, now!"* I think into its mind using my mom's skills. *"Eat the damned spider!"*

Resistant at first, the crow flies off of her shoulder and into our back yard not a moment too soon. Trapped between the arachnid and Esmeralda I don't have any way of escaping. I also can't let it get to Mama's dog like her other pet did, sending Lexi into a rabid fever that almost killed her and Mama.

"Come back here, my pet!" Esmeralda shouts at the gruesome sight, but it's too late. "What are you doing? No, stop it!" The black widow is now a tasty bedtime snack for her favorite crow. "What did you to my bird, you little bitch?"

She didn't just go there with me. "I'm not a bitch, but I'll sick this one on you if you don't back the hell off."

"You nasty little wench! I'll pay you back tenfold for this!" Defeated for the time being, Esmeralda retreats back inside with her pet flying right behind her.

"Good girl," I say, petting Lexi on the head. I'd never forgive myself if something else happened to her. "Let's finish up and call it a night."

Lexi, still wary of our neighbor, scouts the path leading back to the spirit room ahead of me. I glance across the fence into Esmeralda's back yard and see the crow flying erratically on the back porch. I can't help but laugh at my handiwork. If Esmeralda thinks that trick was nasty, I can't wait until she sees my next move. Tomorrow she'll see just how nasty I can be.

"But no matter what, I refuse to allow this school to make me forget who I am and where I come from."
-Jayd
Drama High, volume 10: Culture Clash

~4~
NASTY

The day before Homecoming is finally here, better known as Voting Day. All of the clubs have been doing the most all day to get innocent bystanders to vote for their candidates. What I didn't realize was that at the last minute the Drama Club did indeed decide to throw their hat in the ring. They missed the deadline for queen, but there was apparently still time to write in candidates for princesses and princes in every grade. To my surprise, Alia's being nominated for senior princess, and Chase, of course, for senior prince. I wonder whose bright idea that was.

KJ, Nigel, and Timothy, another popular and rich athlete, have each been nominated by their respective sponsors for homecoming king. They're having a ball relishing in the attention. Nigel's our nominee from ASU, KJ from ASB, and Timothy's on the ballot from one of the high school fraternities, which are only open to those who can afford it. Even if ASU doesn't have the money that the other clubs have, we have the one thing that money doesn't necessarily need to buy—popularity—and our candidates are among the most popular in the entire school. Now that it's the end of the day, it's left up to fate to decide who the victors will be during tomorrow's game.

It was easy enough to deliver the desserts to Esmeralda, as her favorite godchildren are always sending her gifts of thanks for her misdeeds. All I had to do was use my mom's sight on one of her clients by making an early morning visit to Compton and the rest was automatic. I've never met a daughter of Oshune who could turn down decadent sweets. And just as I thought, Misty dutifully brought a few crème puffs to school this morning and shared them with Cameron at break: it's like giving crack to an addict.

With the Homecoming dance tomorrow after the game, and Jeremy not being the easiest to persuade into social situations, I had a feeling that Esmeralda would prescribe something to help Cameron to convince him otherwise and deliver it through Misty; the crème puffs were just the icing on the cake. Now I just have to wait and see if I put enough do-right in them to keep Esmeralda's will suppressed long enough to check her ass.

"Look, it's Venus Williams, or is it Serena? I always get those two confused. Whichever one's the ball buster in that family, that's you," Reid says, laughing at his own sexist joke.

I love both of the tennis champions who hail from my hood, but I doubt he meant that as a compliment.

"They're both from Compton and brought home the gold, so don't get it twisted," I say, wiping the smile right off of his pasty face. "We will clean house tomorrow night when the Homecoming court's announced. At least you'll have each others shoulder's to cry on."

"In your dreams, Jayd," Laura says, claiming her man's arm. "Nellie's a winner, unlike the girl you picked to put on the ballot this year. As if."

"Laura, stop hating," I say, over her self-proclaimed station as the Queen of South Bay High. "When the crown's passed on to Maggie's head, I'll make sure to tag you in the pic."

"I've got a pic for you to tag," Laura says, pulling up the camera app on her phone. "Oh yeah, I forgot you've already seen this one." The picture of Cameron straddling Jeremy in Europe when we were still a couple never gets old, but she doesn't need to know that.

"Wow, your love life must be in serious peril if you have to keep that image on your phone to get your rocks off."

"Shut up, Jayd," Laura says, unamused. "My love life is just fine. But look who I'm talking to: The Virgin freaking Mary herself."

"I'd rather be a freaking virgin than a voyeuristic freak any day." Laura thinks she's got me pegged because of Nellie's big ass mouth, but what they don't know won't hurt me.

"Damn, Jayd. Still not giving it up?" KJ says with his crew in tow, giving Reid and Laura unsolicited back up. How many haters can one sistah deal with at a time? "You know, your cookies aren't as special as you think."

"They were too special for you when we were together, or have you forgotten how hungry your ass was all the damned time?" I stare down my ex boyfriend, happy to be rid of his bull.

"Damn, shorty. You slick with it, huh?" Zachary, the newest member of KJ's crew says. He's new to South Bay High this year and I guess he's not fully caught up on our past. Otherwise, he'd be silent in my presence like their boys Del and C Money have learned to be over the years.

"You have no idea," I say, tired of the argument.

I turn around and head for the parking lot where I'm meeting Mickey. She's giving me a ride to Compton in exchange for me watching Nickey for an hour while she gets her nails done for the game. Chase left campus at lunchtime to again handle some business. I don't ask about that side of his world because I don't need to know the details. He and Jeremy have been growing and dealing weed since they were Sophomores, and even if their families are well off, for whatever reason they like making money that way.

"Jayd, what took you so long?" Mickey asks. Why is she so impatient all of the damned time? That's one of the reasons she and Nellie used to argue so much.

I've got to get my mom's whip back in order and fast. Truth be told, I'd rather take the bus any day than depend on anyone for a ride. If it weren't for me wanting to spend time with my goddaughter I'd tell Mickey a quick see you later with a few other choice words in between.

"Laura and Reid wanted to wish us well for tomorrow's Homecoming announcement at halftime," I say, closing the passenger's side door in her classic ride. It seems like these older cars were meant to last, and I've never heard of anyone breaking into Mickey's, Chase's or Nigel's cars. Maybe my next ride should be a from the 1970's or earlier.

"Yeah, right," Mickey says, joining the procession out of the front lot. It's a bit overcast but that won't stop the residents of the South Bay from heading to the ocean this afternoon. "I'm going to pick up Nickey from daycare and then head to the shop. What time you gotta be at work again?"

"As long as I'm there before five I should be good."

"Good shit." Mickey pumps up the volume and allows Azealia Banks to blast loudly out of the windows. "Did you hear about that girl in my class this afternoon who got suspended?" Mickey shouts.

"Nope. What happened?" News doesn't travel that fast between the halls unless it's about something really juicy.

"This white chick with issues spit in this other chick's Gatorade when she went to the restroom. And she would've gotten away with it too if one of the new dudes in KJ's crew didn't say something."

"That's pretty disgusting, Mickey," I say, imagining what I would do if someone tried that shit with me. "Thanks for sharing."

"Hey, I just want to make sure you're up to date on the nasty people up here. You know white folks can take shit to a whole other level when they want to."

She's got a point there, but all people have their issues. "Nasty is nasty, Mickey. It doesn't matter the culture, race or religion. And that shit right there is flat out revolting."

"I know, right? And it's all because the chick was hating on the girl's pretty eyes and hair. Oh, as a matter of fact it was that girl you took pity on in the main office. What's her name again?"

"Are you talking about Marcia?" I ask, amazed that Mickey could forget formally meeting her after I introduced them a couple of days ago. This girl's selfishness is amazing.

"Yeah, that's it. Marcia," Mickey says, like she's really going to remember her name this time. "She handled it like a G, though. Me, I would've beat that bitch to the ground."

"But that's just the point, Mickey. She shouldn't have to handle it. What's wrong with people that they have to be so mean to someone they don't even know?" Seeing Marcia bullied by Laura, Nellie, and the rest of the mean rich bitch crew brought back memories of my own torture in elementary school. I had to learn how to fight for myself in Compton. I don't know much about Marcia, but I can tell she's not the fighting kind.

"Why do you ask questions that don't have an answer?" For once Mickey makes perfect sense. "Besides, like I said, she wasn't even fazed by that shit. If I didn't know any better I'd say she was almost expecting the nasty girl to do it. She even smiled when old girl was kicked out of class. It was the best thing that I've seen all week."

"Good for Marcia," I say. But I wonder what Mickey means by expecting it? How could Marcia have known that someone would do something as crazy as spit in her drink, and in class no less?

"For real. I even told Marcia that I always hated that beach-trash skank. She used to toss her dirty blonde hair across my desk, getting my phone all wet and shit. And she smells salty like a can of sardines."

"Well damn, Mickey. Why didn't you say something?" I ask. "How are you going to talk about someone and not to someone? That's fake, Mickey, and you know it."

"Hey, Marcia ain't my girl and that wasn't my fight. You know I'm already on probation," Mickey says, telling the truth. "One more visit to Principal Shepherd's office and I'm not walking with my class. I'll be damned if I waste any more time at that god-for-saken school."

At least Mickey has learned that much. I still think that she was wrong for not speaking up in Marcia's defense. There's something about that girl I just can't put my finger on. Monday I'll figure out a way to quietly grill her a bit and find out more about her. At this point I'm not above probing into her mind by any means necessary. She's got secrets up her sleeve, and the way folks have been switching up after meeting Misty I need to make sure she's not one of Esmeralda's soldiers before befriending her any further.

Mickey should know better than to come to Coco's Cosmetology on a Friday afternoon even if she is a regular customer. The place is packed in both the front hair salon and the back nail spa. If they didn't have so many flat screen televisions inside they'd probably be able to move customers in and out a lot quicker. Rather than sit inside of the congested shop, we've opted to sit outside at one of the picnic tables belonging to the barbeque spot two doors down. The food smells delicious but my funds are tight this month. I have to save up for the deductible on my mom's car insurance and every penny counts.

"I need to get my tracks tightened while I'm inside but I don't have time," Mickey says, slapping the back of her head. "It itches so much when it grows out."

"What you need to do is take those tracks out and let your scalp breathe," I say, playing with my god baby. It's been a minute since I hugged my psychic sidekick.

"Everybody can't rock their hair natural like you, Jayd. Hell, my mama told me that I couldn't learn how to drive until I paid for my own perm."

"What the hell does one have to with the other?" I ask, completely confused by her comment. But a lot of what her family does baffles me. For example, allowing Mickey's always-fresh-out-of-the-penitentiary boyfriend to spend the night at their full house is one of those things that I'll never understand.

"It has to do with maturity. If I'm grown enough to drive I should be grown enough to take care of my own hair, right? I can't be walking around with a nappy head claiming to be a grown ass woman."

My god baby looks at her mother the same way I'm looking at her: this chick is so, so hood.

"If you say so. Just don't expose the baby to those poisonous fumes inside the shop," or on her head, but I'm going to stop myself from saying that thought out loud. Mickey doesn't like it when I overstep my bounds with her baby.

"Jayd, you're always such a damn worrywart," Mickey says, looking toward the shop. "That's why your ass will never be able to give it up to nobody. If you keep acting like that, you're going to die a virgin."

I stop short of checking Mickey with the truth, but me and Chase know that there would be little benefit to telling our friends about us. And Mickey wouldn't be able to keep it a secret for too long. It would be nice to have someone to share it with, but my options are very limited.

"Uh oh," I say, as the pacifier falls from Nickey's mouth to the sidewalk.

"I got it." Mickey reclaims the pacifier and puts it down on the table without attempting to rinse it with her bottled water. Before I know it, Nickey picks it up and puts it back in her mouth without missing a beat.

"Mickey, why didn't you rinse it off first?" I ask, taking the binky from Nickey who truly could care less. I think she's teething and just wants something to suck on for comfort.

"She's okay. I do that all the time and she ain't never been sick."

"Mickey, the three-second rule doesn't apply to babies you know." I hold Nickey close to me and rinse the pacifier myself before putting it in her diaper bag. If she asks for it I'll give it to her. Mama always says to let a baby develop independent habits, meaning don't give her a pacifier just out of habit, and to put her down on her belly more often rather than holding her or putting her in a walker all of the time like Mickey's mama does.

"You think I don't know how to take care of my own daughter, Jayd? You sound just like Nigel, damn." Mickey stands up to reach for Nickey who's comfortably playing in my lap just as one of the stylists calls her name. "I'll be back."

"And we'll be here." When she's safely out of earshot, I focus all of my attention on Nickey and she does the same to me. We need to catch up on a few things. *"That's just nasty, Nickey. Don't ever take a pacifier if it's not clean."* I know she can't talk yet but she definitely understands what I'm saying.

Nickey smiles up at me showing off her pretty gums. She touches one of the remaining jade bracelets on my wrist without taking her eyes off of mine.

"Long time no dream, godmama," Nickey says *from her mind into mine. I forgot how sassy this little girl can be. It's been a minute since we psychically chatted.*

"I missed you too, Nickey," I smile. *"So what's on your mind? Similac, Sesame Street, Dora the Explorer?"*

"Oh, I see you got mad jokes when you know this isn't the time or place for it. What are you doing to make sure my parents get back together? Seems like you've been sleeping on the job lately."

"Nickey, I have no control over what Mickey and Nigel do or don't do in this case," I say. *"Have you ever thought that maybe, just maybe, they're not supposed to be together and you can still be raised by them both?"*

"That's not an option, godmama Jayd. Not an option!" This little girl is too much, just like her mama. I can't wait to see what's she's like at sixteen. *"Let me show you what's going to happen if you don't do something about it and fast."*

Nickey takes me through her sight where I see Mickey suffering a serious identity crisis, a leftover side effect of the post-partum depression pills Esmeralda gave her months ago, which did more damage than I originally thought. As a result, Mickey decides to allow Nigel's mom to keep Nickey and runs off with G who ends up killing Esmeralda after finding out that she's been manipulating him out of money for months.

"See, I told you. You've got work to do on my behalf, and the sooner the better. Please and thank you," Nickey says as she releases my bracelet.

Nickey's right; I need to take this custody battle between her parents more seriously than I have been, even if her parents are acting like kids themselves. Again, I say it would be best if I could just make a few dolls to help my friends act right. Life would be so much easier, but unfortunately that's not an option.

Why is there always something else to do? I don't know how Cameron, Misty or Esmeralda have responded to my dessert yet and now I have to get to work on Mickey's silly self. How will I ever be able to find a minute to focus on my needs long enough to resolve some of my own issues?

I'll have to check the spirit book for the choices that I do have and will talk it over with Netta and Mama, if she's in her right mind, when I get to the shop in a little while. Until then, it's naptime for my little supernatural diva.

"Besides, all that glitters is not gold."
-Jayd
Drama High, volume 2: Second Chance

~ 5 ~
# ONCE BITTEN, TWICE FLYY

"Calling me nappy-headed is tantamount to calling me a nigga, and I don't answer to either," Netta says, placing the fresh laundry on an empty drier chair for me to fold. I caught them up on my conversation with Mickey earlier this afternoon and it's been a hot topic ever since.

"I don't think it's that bad, Netta," I say. I've been busy since I walked through the door. It was nice to have her sisters here to help out over the past few weeks while Mama was out of commission, but unfortunately they have a tendency to rearrange the shop and mess up our pre-established flow. "And depending on who's calling you a nigga it could be a term of endearment, not an insult."

"The hell it ain't," Netta says, not giving me any leeway." You're too young to remember those days, but I'm here to tell you that as a child of the sixties after nappy-headed was always followed by nigga, and sometimes a noose after that."

The three customers in the shop nod their heads in agreement. How can they even hear? One is getting her hair washed by Mama and the other two are under the driers.

"I still give the young folks credit for taking the heat out of a very powerful word and making it their own," Mama says, giving me the out I was looking for from Netta. Usually she's my savior but not on this subject. "Ain't nothing like taking ignorant folks' language and throwing it back at them."

"Thank you, Mama. That's all I'm trying to say." I wink at my godmother who winks back at me. I know she's just giving me a hard time out of love. "I don't always agree with it but I understand the purpose."

"To me it's all ignorant," Netta says, checking her clients' hair to see if they're dry. She turns the timer on for another 5 minutes on both driers and continues. "That's like when we went through rush week during our freshmen year, Lynn Mae. You remember that bull they made us go through?"

"Yes, Lord. They are very into the uniformed appearance, that's for sure," Mama answers. "Each sorority had its own distinct look. You could tell who was what a mile away."

"And Alpha Gamma Rho girls were all pretty, distinguished, and had bone-straight hair. And with those green eyes of hers your grandmother fit in perfectly with the kind of girl they were looking to recruit."

"Oh Netta, please. So were you." Mama takes her client to her station to blow her hair out. These are our last clients for the evening. Unlike at Mickey's shop, at Netta's Never Nappy Beauty Shop we get them in and out as efficiently as possible. Time is money in more ways than one.

"Well, all I know is that by the end of that week I had decided to stay Me Phi Me and your grandmother was unofficially on line with the sisterhood." Netta still has more than a little salt to throw regarding Mama's ill-fated decision. It's hard to believe that Mama and Teresa Esop were ever friends let alone sorority sisters.

"In my eyes I was going with Oshune's sisterhood, which wasn't such a bad thing, Netta," Mama says, stating her reasoning. Her client's almost asleep because of the expert way my grandmother can run a rolling brush through her hair with one hand and blow dry it with the other. By the time Mama's done, her hair will be shiny, bouncy, and full of body—all without heavy heat.

"But it was just the opposite wasn't it, honey?" Netta says, freeing the first client from the drier. "Instead, you messed around and ended up with a bunch of Erzulie Fredas to deal with, and the worst part is that they didn't even know who they were. Can you imagine a bunch of Esmeraldas walking around campus thinking that they owned the place?

Girl, please!"

"No, I can't." I shudder at the thought of multiple Esmeraldas. Even one is too much for this world.

"You're all done, Mrs. Parker," Netta says, taking the drape from around the elderly lady's shoulders and shaking it out.

"Perfection as usual," Mrs. Parker says, eyeing herself in the mirror at Netta's station. "Here you are, dear. This is for me and Julia." Mrs. Parker hands Netta the money who promptly walks it over to the shrine behind the front door and places the four twenty-dollar bills there.

"Thank you so much, honey," Netta says, walking back over to the drier and freeing Mrs. Parker's sister.

"See you next week, Nancy," Mama says to her client who hands her cash as well. "Remember what I told you about wearing your scarf too tight at night. It's wreaking havoc on your edges." Mama signals for me to come over and claim the money for the larger shrine in the office. "When you go back there get one of the samples we whipped up this morning and give it to Mrs. Nancy. It'll help with her regrowth process."

"Yes, ma'am." I do as I'm told while the women say their goodbyes like they've been doing for as long as I can remember. Netta and Mama's clients are as loyal as they come.

76

"Well that sure was a productive day," Netta says, locking the front door. "Let's finish our discussion over dinner. I don't know about y'all but I'm going to need some more energy to clean up this place."

"I couldn't agree more," Mama says, washing her hands.

"I'll get the food out and warm it up."

I follow Netta to the back porch where the intimate kitchen is housed. Just like in Mama's spirit room, culinary miracles are created in here.

"As I was saying, your Mama messed up when she joined those witches." Netta says, picking up right where we left off. "And boy did they work their magic on her back in the day." Netta shakes her head at the memory.

"Oh Netta, you can be so dramatic," Mama says, pulling out a chair and sitting down.

I set the plates and silverware down on the table and claim a chair of my own. "So what really went down with you and Teresa?" I ask, ever curious about their relationship. Me and Nigel have a lot in common, but his mother and my grandmother, not so much.

"At the time she was my line sister, my soon to be sands," Mama says. "That's a special relationship. Once you're on line together you're bonded for life, or so the saying goes."

"She was never your sister, Lynn Mae," Netta says, dishing out the hot food. They both threw down last night and brought it too work. Lucky me. "Sisters don't judge you or try to change you or smile in your face while trying to literally push you off of a cliff."

"Netta, that wasn't the entire story." The scents of fried chicken and rice permeate the air, making my stomach growl. It's been a minute since I had a good home cooked meal even if we're technically not at home. "No, we were never truly sisters, but just because I had a bad experience doesn't mean that the entire sorority experience is a bad one to have. You just have to be very careful about who you trust. That goes for all situations."

"What your grandmother is failing to tell you for some reason are the horrors of pledging that she experienced via those jealous wenches," Netta says. Netta must sense that something's way off with Mama too. She's just being too nice about things that she would usually be up in arms about.

"I'm not failing to tell the girl a thing," Mama says. "I'm simply choosing my words more carefully these days. I know you remember your lessons about keeping a cool head, my little fire child?" Mama winks at me.

"Jayd, sometimes it's okay to go off on a person if it's completely justifiable, as should've been the case with your grandmother and those women," Netta says, full of steam herself. "Cool head my ass."

Mama looks at her best friend in almost utter disbelief. She knows Netta like no one else ever could, yet these best friends can still shock the hell out of each other.

"Teresa was the president of our line and I was the ace, the first one in line," Mama says.

"And your grandmother was also the most rebellious. Don't forget to tell her that, Lynn Mae," Netta shouts from the front of the shop.

"Can I tell the story please, Netta? You weren't a witness to everything, you know?"

"I'm just filling in the blanks, Lynn Mae. That's all."

Mama looks over her shoulder toward the sink area and waits for Netta to reappear so that she can give her the eye roll of her life. Netta probably knows this and is deliberately taking her time to come back.

"I had a dream of Olokun warning me about crossing the burning sands with my so-called sisters. When I woke up I called each of my line sisters and warned them about my vision. They laughed it off and called it a nightmare, nothing more. One of the big sisters even teased me about it at that night's session. She made me sing that song 'Sweet Dreams' by the Erythmitics every time she called my name. It was a

79

long night."

"It wasn't nothing sweet about that dream, child." Netta pokes her head around the wall shared between the back porch and the interior hallway. "And do you think those wenches listened to your grandmother? Ha!" Netta shakes her finger at Mama before disappearing back into the shop.

"Anyhow, that night I had the same dream and this time I shared it with my sisters since they wouldn't believe my words. It wasn't intentional except for that I wished for them to heed the warning. Somehow it got through to each of them. I've never had a mass dream with others like that again. Still, they didn't take it seriously and went to the session that night anyway."

"Stupid girls." Netta finally reemerges carrying money, Florida water, a large brass comb, and a fan.

"I chose not to show up that night and caught the full wrath of my big sisters the next day. One thing you don't do is miss a session when on line. Unfortunately, before I could talk to my sisters I was abruptly removed from the line and pledged solo for the next couple of weeks. During that time my dreams grew even more intense. I couldn't share them with the others no matter how hard I tried to will it to happen again. I think that they shut me out because they were afraid."

"Stupid, stupid girls." Netta shakes her head at the memory.

"I had a different dream one night, as if everything that I'd been dreaming for weeks was in the distant past including the events of that night. I wasn't invited to that final pledge session but I was there anyway in spirit. Along with everyone else present, except for my line sisters who were blindfolded and kneeling at the ocean's shore, I watched in horror as two of my line sisters drowned to death in the rough waters. It happened so fast. One minute they were arm-in-arm with the rest of the pledges, the next they were being carried away by a rip tide."

"Horrible those women had to lose their lives like that. And nobody helped them. Not a single one of those so-called brothers or sisters tried to save those girls."

"No one knew how to swim, Netta," Mama says, defensively. I've never heard her cut them any slack before.

Netta and Mama remain silent for a moment, each of them personally reliving the memory in their own way. It must've been horrible for Mama knowing that had they listened to her those women would've survived.

I'm glad I haven't told Mama about Alpha Gamma Rho's scholarship arrangement. I don't want to feel the wrath of Netta, and I also want Mama to be back one-hundred when I do let her know that the money I won during the cotillion were my educational funds to keep with strings attached, of course.

"If you ever want to pledge a sorority, Jayd, I recommend that you wait until you graduate, get to know the girls first. There are good organizations out there doing amazing work."

"I say you can do all of that by your damn self. You don't need Greek letters to do good work." Netta's unrelenting of her hatred for anything organized, especially if it takes away her best friend and business partner's attention. "When you go to college you should have fun and enjoy the process. And remember to keep your guard up at all times. The same women who smile at you will also secretly plot your demise."

"That can be true," Mama agrees. "Trust me, if they are truly meant to be your sisters, like a good man, it'll wait until you graduate."

"I know about trusting a new sistah friend too quickly, like Misty for example." I shudder at the memory of us ever being best friends.

"That's the thing with Misty. She's not bad but she has been taught to thrive in chaos and that is not in harmony with her true nature," Mama says, taking a bite of her chicken. "I remember her as a sweet child with great spiritual potential at one time but the women around her live for creating drama. We are at war with that energy, not necessarily the people that possess it. They have been taught wrong and it is up to is to

make it right."

"Some people are too far gone to come back to the right side," I

say, sprinkling more hot sauce on my food.

"Do you remember your ceremony?" Mama says. How could I

ever forget that night? "After the bitter always comes the sweet. Have

faith in the sweet, Jayd. Hold out for the sweet."

"What happened with you and Daddy back in the day?" I ask,

easing into my interrogation of their rekindled fire. Maybe Netta can

help me get to the bottom of Mama's strange behavior with her own line

of questioning.

"Esmeralda, that's what," Netta says. She pours more iced tea for

the three of us and I gladly accept the refreshment. It's a bit stuffy back

here.

"I should've known." I can't help but smile at the memory of

Esmeralda's face when I convinced her bird to eat her spider. She

deserves everything that's coming to her. Turning her pets against each

other was just the beginning.

"Dr. Whitmore and I had an affair many years ago, more

emotional than anything," Mama confesses matter-of-factly. "But yes, it

was physical too. Esmeralda found out and held it against me for as long as she could. Eventually I just didn't give a damn anymore, and of course she ran and told your grandpa the first chance she got."

"That Esmeralda's a piece of work, honey!" Netta says, shaking the excess water from her tools. "Your grandpa was hot, chile, but really he couldn't say shit since he'd been having numerous liaisons for years."

Mama cuts her eyes at Netta and continues. "Even still your grandfather was crushed, especially when he found out that it was our family doctor, the very same doctor that I was in love with way back when."

Kinda like Chase would be if he found out that I'm still carrying a torch for Rah no matter how subconscious the flame might be. "How do you know when it's time to stop loving someone?"

"Once you're in love you never really stop loving that person," Netta says, fanning the brass comb dry. "It's just relationship shit, Jayd. That's all I can say about that."

"It's kind of like when you can't explain the emotions you're feeling inside of your own head. There are no words for it, Jayd. Dr. Whitmore and I have a bond that cannot be broken, nor should it ever be. Mama stands to clear the rest of the dishes from the table. We also recognize that we can never be involved on that level yet we still have a destiny to live out with the other never too far away. We can be good together in more ways than one. You know when it is time to stay and when it is time to leave." Mama's on point with that statement.

"And that's why I had to intervene back then, just like I had to do this time around," Netta says, smiling at me in between sips of her sweet tea.

"What do you mean intervene?" I look at Netta and try to probe her mind but she just continues to smile and touches Mama's hairpin. I noticed it when she first came home from Dr. Whitmore's office but didn't really think anything of it. I thought it was a gift from him.

"The old witch doctor's bag of tricks helped to keep Rousseau off of your grandmother's tracks, but Esmeralda's dark magic had already begun to take hold of your grandmother's head. So I made her a little protection of my own."

I never thought of Netta as one to go rogue when it came to the spiritual work. She always works in conjunction with Mama but I guess when she has to she can work it out just fine by herself.

"Is this also the reason behind Mama's rekindled attraction to her husband?"

"Yes, it is. But it's not a trick, Jayd. Esmeralda got into Lynn Mae's head and turned her dreams upside down." I do remember the unfortunate dreams as I was right there tripping with her. "Notice the tiny reflection in the pin? That keeps whatever Esmeralda did off of your grandmother's crown. Among other sweet blessings, your grandmother no longer feels animosity towards her mate because all of that heat was created by Esmeralda, too."

"And I couldn't be happier, honey." Mama's mischievous smile lets me know that she's fully aware of what her best friend's been up to. "As a matter of fact, I feel like a little something sweet. Do we still have that pastry dough from last night?"

"Yes, indeed," Netta says, excited. "It's in the fridge.

"Excellent," Mama says. "A strawberry tart should do the trick."

"My favorite," Netta says. She walks over to the cupboard where the dishes are housed and takes out a baking pan, ready to help.

"All in all I made a lot of mistakes with men, but being with Dr. Whitmore wasn't one of them. He used to always say that I saved him from his own demons, and I'd like to think that was a mutual good deed. We probably would have been married but he doesn't believe in God, kids, or marriage. He is a straight up Ogun man, so I married Shango man instead—a typical Oshune woman I am."

"What do you mean you saved him from his demons?" I wonder if Rah feels that way about me.

"Well baby, he didn't take it lightly when I became pregnant with your mama," Mama says. "We weren't together any more and I think he felt guilty about not being able to step up to the plate like your granddaddy eventually did."

It's common knowledge that Daddy isn't the father of all of Mama's children but we never talk about it. He also has children other than the kids he has with mama, so I guess the playing field is level in that way.

"Erzulie has many paths, like all of the loas, orishas, saints; whatever you want to call them. And not all of them are good," Netta says, moving on to the next task on her never-ending to-do list. "Esmeralda has chosen to worship a path of pure vanity, thus her youthful appearance. But it's a mirage, Jayd, just like everything else that she does. Esmeralda can only mirror ashe, never truly possess it herself."

"How can y'all be so calm when you now that Esmeralda's always gunning for us?" This discussion's pissing me off even more.

"Child, it's one thing to keep your cool when the world around you is peaceful. It's a whole other kind of strength to have a calm and focused mind while in the eye of a storm," Mama says, molding the dough with her right hand. That tart is going to be so damn good, starting with that crust. "Always feed your faith to starve your fears."

How does she know just what to do and say all of the time?

"*She does it because she's Mama*," my mom says, comfortable settling into my thoughts as the evening dies down.

I put her bracelet back on this morning while Mama's still healing. I might need to chat it up with my mom on occasion. It's nice to have the option, at least until they both notice the block out.

"That's a nice iPod, Jayd," Netta says, noticing the new but old device on my hip. I never realized how much of my phone battery is wasted playing music. This little thing is already coming in handy.

"It was a gift from Jeremy," I admit. "Truth be told I feel guilty keeping it, especially since we're not together anymore and I'm dealing with Chase now." Not to mention my naughty dreams with Rah, but one confession at a time. "I tried to give it back but of course he wouldn't take it."

"Don't feel guilty about material things," Mama says. "Stuff is easy to get. The more challenging thing is to ask into the universe for good friends, love, health—all of the stuff that money can't buy. True wealth has to be manifested internally, and material wealth externally. It's the natural order of things. And sometimes you have to work with what you've got until you get what it is that you truly want."

And there it is. The truth of the matter is that shit isn't as bad with me and Chase as I'm making it out to be. As long as I take it in stride and not allow my past to dictate my present we should be good. Is it a normal boyfriend/girlfriend relationship: no. But I don't need one of those right now anyway, and if he's truthful about it, neither does Chase. The last thing we need is people all up in our shit. Just like the paparazzi and social media, it's fun when it's good and hell when it's bad. I don't know about Chase, but I'd rather stay on the lighter side of life as much as I can for the moment. The heavy stuff comes all on its own and usually without warning.

"Sometimes the people you think are your friends can be worse than enemies."
-Lynn Marie
Drama High, volume 4: Frenemies

~6~
WON'T YOU COME?

"Thank you so much for making this for me on such short notice," I say, admiring Mama's handiwork in the mirror. The green dress is perfect for tonight's dance. I may not be on the court but in this outfit I will surely feel royal.

"Anything for my baby," Mama says, standing behind me in the floor-length mirror. *"Here, this pearl necklace will compliment your neckline perfectly."*

"It's beautiful." Mama secures the clasp at the back of my neck and rests her hands on my shoulders. I catch her green eyes in the mirror and they begin to glow before turning an icy blue.

"Come home, my daughter. Come home!" The blue light moves out of the mirror and takes over the entire room. I attempt to move out of the reflection but can't escape the cold glare.

"Let go of me!" I scream, but Mama laughs an evil laugh and is unrelenting in her grasp on my body.

"Never, mi petite," she says, sounding more like Rousseau than herself. *"You know that you belong with us. Won't you come?"*

Mama's red nails grow into claws and begin to dig into my skin. The red polish and my blood collide causing me to loose sight of where her claws end and my flesh begins.

"Never! You can't have me!" I scream into the reflection. Damn she's strong.

"Oh, it's not you that I want, my precious. Just your blood."

"So be it." I glare back into the mirror and summon Maman's powers into my sight. If they want my blood they're going to get it and then some.

"What are you doing to me?" Esmeralda says through my grandmother. "You wouldn't want to hurt your grandmother would you?"

"I could never do that, Esmeralda. And besides, our blood's too strong for your veins." The tattoo on my arm of our family veve heats up. Before she can let go, I grab her hands and force her nails deeper into my flesh. I've got her now.

"No!" she shrieks. "Marie, you evil bitch! Let me go!"

"You should know by now that we don't take orders from you, especially not my great-grandmother." I can feel the blood coursing through my veins and into hers. This isn't the kind of transfusion she was going for, I'm sure. But she should know our blood types don't mix; it's on her that her body's rejecting it.

91

"You'll see, Jayd, soon enough. Join me or die!" And just like that, Esmeralda's gone and I'm left alone to clean up her mess. So much for wearing my royal gown.

Last night's dream was unsettling, mostly because it reminded me that I have nothing to wear to homecoming tonight. Instead of working at the shop this morning I went to Simply Wholesome to train under Summer. I finally agreed to her apprentice hours and to get this training over with sooner rather than later. I wish I could say no to money but I'm not in that position at the moment. My mom was thrilled but I haven't had a chance to run it by Mama and Netta yet. With Mama's good mood I doubt she'd object.

Chase and I decided to go to the Westside Pavilion to shop for Homecoming gear since we're already on this side of town. It's nice to have a friend who'll not only pick up a sistah from work, but also to go shopping with.

"I still can't believe you'd rather go to homecoming by yourself than with your boy," Chase says, flipping through the stylish clothes. We've been at the mall for over an hour and I still haven't found a dress to wear tonight. I was perfectly satisfied with wearing something already hanging in my mother's closet but Chase wouldn't hear of it.

He's not really into the whole homecoming court thing but he still wants to look flyy to represent the Drama Club and says that I should do the same for ASU.

"Chase, come on. We've talked about this a million times over," I say, taking a shirt from the rack and holding it up to Chase's chest. "We cannot be seen in public together as a couple, especially not at a formal event all cuddled up and shit."

"You mean like this?" Chase embraces me tightly and picks me up off the ground. "Mmmm, you smell good."

"So do you." Normally I would playfully slap his arm and demand that he put me down but I don't want him to let go of me just yet. I don't think that we were expecting to catch such strong feelings for each other but that's exactly what's happening.

"See, we're a good smelling couple. We have to go to the homecoming together. It's meant to be." Chase smiles down at me and kisses my forehead before putting my feet back on the ground.

"I feel you, but it's going to be too obvious that we're more than friends if we show up together."

I straighten out my clothes, replace the now wrinkled shirt onto the rack, and lead the way toward Nordstrom. It's one of the only stores where I know we can both find something cute to wear and fast. I have a lot to do before tonight and don't want us to get stuck in West LA traffic.

"Jayd, it's homecoming, not prom. But I wouldn't mind escorting you to that, too." Chase takes my left hand in his right and massages between my fingers. It would be nice to walk freely hand in hand with Chase but it's too soon for that.

"Chase, you're real touchy-feely today for somebody who agreed to keep things on the low for the time being," I say, giving him a gentle squeeze and then letting go to search through the sales rack. All I need is something simple and cute to wear that will represent the club and Maggie properly, even if all eyes will be on my girl when she walks onto the football field at halftime. She's keeping her dress under wraps but I know that she's going to look good in whatever she wears, just like Nellie. One thing they definitely have in common is their sense of style.

"What if I don't want to keep us a secret anymore? Could you handle that?" Chase takes a sexy yet elegant red dress not hanging on a sales rack and holds it up in front of me. He nods his head affirmatively.

"Chase, I don't know," I say, almost whining. "Don't we have enough drama in our lives as it is?" I take the lovely dress from him and consider it momentarily until I see the price tag. Back on the rack it goes. It must be nice to shop with no limit.

"There's always going to be drama in life, Jayd. That's just how it is."

While I think of a sound argument to his reasoning I spot drama coming around the corner. "Oh shit," I say, claiming a dress from the rack without truly considering it.

"What?" Chase turns around. His eyes follow mine as he sighs at the sight. "What are Nellie and Cameron doing all the way out here?"

"This is one of Nellie's favorite malls. And because the broad still can't drive, I assume Cameron's her ride."

Unfortunately they've made eye contact and are heading this way.

"Aren't you two a sight for sore eyes," Cameron says. She sounds like she's watched one too many episodes of *Nashville*.

"Whatever, Cameron," I say, rolling my eyes at the fake wench. "Let me guess. You're shopping for clothes to dress up another voodoo doll?"

A few of the other customers look at us sideways. The last thing I want is to be caught up in a mall scene this afternoon.

"Jayd, please," Nellie says, looking at her ex-boyfriend. "The real question is what are you two doing here? Don't you have a girlfriend to attend to or did Jayd scare her off, too?"

"Jayd didn't scare anyone off," Chase says, putting his arm around my shoulders. "That's more your mode of operation, wouldn't you say?"

"Go to hell, Chase," Nellie sneers at him.

"I just got back from there, actually," Chase says, standing erect and folding his arms across his chest. "Your daddy said to tell you hi."

"Okay, it's been nice chatting," I say, reaching for Chase's left hand. We need to leave this situation before it gets out of control. I know that it's hard to have any sympathy for Nellie, but she's in way over her head with Cameron. I think she can't see which way is up anymore.

"You know, you two look awfully cozy these days to be just friends friend, as you always say." Cameron's an evil bitch for throwing that out there, and in front of Nellie no less. Maybe she didn't take a big enough bite of the crème puffs. She's one of those broads who's always on a diet.

Nellie looks from Chase to me as the thought sinks into her brain.

"As usual Cameron, your paranoia has gotten the best of what little sense you do have," I say, but I can tell Nellie's not buying it. "I know you don't know what true friendship looks like since you're into manipulating by any means necessary to get a friend, but we're real friends. Ever had one?"

"You don't need to explain anything to these two," Chase says, reclaiming my shoulders. "And what if we are together? That would be our business, not yours."

I could kill Chase for planting that seed even deeper into Nellie's mind. Damn it.

"Are you capable of finding your own man or do always have to steal someone else's?" Who does Nellie think she's talking to? The next time she finds herself in trouble she'd better not call me for help. I'm done turning the other cheek in our friendship.

"Nellie, you need to check yourself before you get thoroughly embarrassed in front of all of these people up in here today." I'm trying to give her the benefit of the doubt. After all I've done for this girl she's decided to take sides with my latest enemy. Too bad for her that the wrath of Jayd is ready to rain down on all bitches, including her if she doesn't calm her ass down.

"Let's get out of here, Jayd," Chase says, this time being the one to lead the way out of the fire. "We've got better shit to do."

"We'll see you two tonight," Cameron says after us. "And make sure to match your colors. Couples always look so cute when they do. Jeremy and I are wearing blue, so you may want to choose something different."

I glare at Cameron over my shoulder tempted to make her head explode with a vicious migraine, but Maman's powers are nothing to play with. She's lucky that I have some self-control because if I didn't, instead of being gentle in my approach with the crème puffs I'd have to go full throttle on her ass, to hell with the consequences.

"See, what did I tell you?" Chase says. He steps aside so that I can walk through the automatic glass doors ahead of him. "We should just let it out. The vibe is already out there and I'm not ashamed of it."

Why is he so eager to invite even more bull into our lives? "Chase, it's not out there but you sure are doing your best to release it every chance you get."

"Would it be so bad to officially be my girl, Jayd?"

"I don't know," I say, almost to the car. "Why don't you ask your best friend Jeremy and get back to me?"

"I can't believe you're still worried about him. Why don't you just admit that you want him back and be done with it?"

"Because that's not true. Not at all." I sit down and he slams the car door behind me.

"Well then what is it? Nellie and Jeremy are big people, just like us. They can handle it." Chase closes his door and puts the key into the ignition without turning it. He sits back hard in the driver's seat and laughs slightly. "Oh, I don't know why I didn't think about it before," Chase says, finally starting the engine. "It's Rah."

"No, Chase. It's not anyone." At least not outside of my dreams.

"Forget I said anything, Jayd. From what I know you've never lied to me before. I don't want you to start today."

I'm too hurt by his words to protest.

Without waiting for a response, Chase pulls away from the parking space and allows a patient driver to replace his car. "You want to hit up Melrose while we're out here? We might be able to find something there."

"Sure." I know he's pissed and frustrated but I'm just not willing to deal with hurting multiple folks at the same time. That's got to lead to bad karma. I don't know about Chase, but I can't afford anymore negative energy.

I wish I could go to the Homecoming Dance with Chase as his girl. I wish that Nigel and Mickey would stop fighting and amicably figure out what they want. I wish I could stop dreaming about being with Rah. Most of all, I wish that wishing was a viable solution to all of our problems. It feels like my world is shattering all around me and I don't know how to pick up all of the pieces.

*"Boys don't know how to court girls, and girls don't know how to make
boys work for it anymore."*
-Netta
Drama High, volume 11: Cold As Ice

~ 7 ~
GLASS HOUSES

When we got back to Chase's house, Mrs. Carmichael was at their neighbor's house sipping wine and involved in a deep discussion about world affairs on the front porch. Chase and I decided to take a nap before getting dressed but neither of us could sleep. There was too much tension in the air—both emotional and sexual.

Without saying a word I kissed Chase and he responded. For the first time this evening, Chase and I made love in complete silence. I do love Chase and think he's an attractive dude. I'm just not sure how to reconcile my brotherly love toward him into seeing him as my man. In the meantime I'm enjoying what our friendship has morphed into, even though I know it may have to end soon if we can't agree on our limitations.

We both found something to wear to tonight's festivities, after which we plan on going to a party with Maggie's folks, including the ones she has in common with Chase. It's time for me to call in the street soldiers to handle Esmeralda while the effect of the crème puffs is still in tact. I'm not exactly sure how long the protection will last, which is why we must act swiftly.

I have no doubt that we'll also be celebrating Maggie's victory tonight. So far Nigel's been having one hell of a night on the football field with the game against our biggest rival tied. There are only two minutes left in the first half and then the real games can begin.

"Jayd, that outfit is mui caliente, honey," Maggie says, playfully smacking my hip.

I have to admit that I'm also feeling the chic, nude-colored jumpsuit and heels to match. With my hair pulled back and lip-gloss popping, I do feel rather cute.

"Thank you, chica. And look at you," I say, admiring her gown. She looks stunning in a sophisticated, form-fitting white gown with red pumps to match her lips.

"If looks could kill all of those other brujas would be six-feet deep by now," Mario says. He eases his arms around her waist and pulls Maggie down into his lap. It seems like we've been waiting in the gym for hours. Each club has their own station to wait for our candidates' cues.

"Yes. If only." This afternoon's run in with Cameron and Nellie was enough to test his theory but then I would've missed the opportunity to see their faces when Maggie's crowned Homecoming Queen. That's as close as I want to get to their ultimate demise tonight.

"It's time! It's time!" one of the Freshman ASB groupies shouts into the crowded gymnasium. Kendra's right by his side quickly gathering their nominees together, including Nellie.

"Let's get it," I say, waving to the Drama Club as they make their way across the crowded gymnasium. Alia touches Chase's arm and he bends his elbow like the perfect escort that he is. Normally he wouldn't want anything to do with his jealous ex, but I guess tonight he's feeling charitable—at least I hope that's all that he's feeling for her.

All of the candidates and supporters check their selves out one more time before lining up to walk across the stage.

"We'll begin with the freshman class and make our way up," Reid says to the enthusiastic crowd.

"Sorry about the sweat ladies. You see I'm out there doing my thang," Nigel says, wrapping his arms around Maggie's shoulders and then mine.

"Yuck, Nigel," I say, removing his sweaty, muscular arm from my neck. "You could've changed first."

102

"Girl please," he says, pinching my right cheek. "This is that good funk. The funk of victory." As usual, my boy is cocky and hyped for his role as quarterback.

"And for your senior class court the nominees are," Reid announces. He takes the cue cards from Laura and continues to read.

Maggie and Nigel smile at each other before meeting in the center of the stage with the other nominees.

"And now, your king and queen of homecoming are none other than..."

"Stop playing and read the damn card," someone shouts from the crowd.

I scan the bleachers and see that it's one of the surfer crew members. Jeremy would normally be with them if here at all, but whatever Esmeralda gave Cameron worked like the charm that it was. Jeremy's here with the chick and in his matching blue shirt, just like she said they would be. I've got to hand it to Mama's nemesis, she does have some skills. That will make kicking her ass all the sweeter.

"Maggie and KJ, come on down!"

KJ? Damn. I should've prayed harder for our boy to win, but oh well. At least Maggie's queen: that's all that really matters.

Nellie looks absolutely devastated as the crown passes right by her. She looks off stage and dead at me. If my former friend didn't hate me before she sure does now.

After South Bay High's winning game, Nigel, Nellie, and the rest of the runner-ups are officially crowned as a part of the Homecoming court.

"Congratulations everyone! It's picture time," Kendra announces, directing the court on stage.

"Places, everyone! Please couple up accordingly," the same overly excited ASB groupie says to the court. "Club sponsors will also have a chance to take a photo with their nominees."

"Congratulations, Nellie." Nigel pulls Nellie into his chest and holds her tight.

"You too, Nigel." Nellie looks like she's ready to break down but holds it together. I know she takes losing hard but I have a feeling that her tears are about more than a crown.

"Yeah, Nellie. Congratulations," Maggie says, being a good sport.

Nigel let's go off Nellie and her eyes immediately dart from side to side. Who's she looking for?

"Thank you, Maggie. I have to go," Nellie says, walking quickly toward the exit.

"You should come to the after party, Nellie," Nigel yells after her but she's out of earshot.

"I'm sure Nellie will be hanging out with her new crew," I say, shaking my head in disappointment. I wish I could see Cameron but she's somewhere in the crowd.

"Well, you're welcome to celebrate with us, Nigel," Maggie says, taking off her crown and placing it on her little sister's head. "We're going to my cousin Pete's house in Manhattan Beach. You should all come and eat."

"I'm always down with that," Nigel says, putting his arm around my shoulders.

Chase looks on as we walk toward the back exit leading out into the parking lot.

"Are you coming?" I ask, concerned about my friend. I hope he's not starting to resent being with me. I don't mean to hurt him but I'm just not ready to be anyone's girl yet, especially not with all of the problems that us being together would cause.

"Yeah, Chase. Let's get our eat on, man." Nigel, unaware of Chase's melancholy mood, tries to persuade him but I don't think that Chase is up to partying tonight.

"I'll catch up to you later, man. I've got some business I have to handle first, but I know where you're at." Chase looks down at his vibrating cell and quickly returns the text. "Save me a plate."

"Sure thing, papi," Maggie says. She takes her little sister's hand with her man behind them both. "Vamanos, people. We've got a crown to celebrate." Her little sister beams with pride, visibly pissing off the competition as we exit the gymnasium.

All in all I'd say it was a pretty successful night. I wanted Nigel to win for king, but he doesn't seem bothered one bit by being crowned a prince. Alia also seems fine with being crowned a princess and is celebrating with the rest of the Drama Club crew. I'll have to make sure to congratulate the club next week.

Chase's happiness is important to me and I feel like for the first time in our entire friendship that I'm causing him pain. But I don't know what to do about it. Hopefully he shows up to Pete's later and we can talk about it without the pressure of being alone. If we could just wipe the slate clean and start over from scratch I would've paid closer attention to his crush on me two years ago. Who knows? We might've still been together to this very day instead of in the strained relationship we're creating. I've got to find a way to make things right between us.

"The masses have more power than a so-called justice system can ever embody."
-Mama
Drama High, volume 15: Street Soldiers

~8~
CLEAN SLATE

"Hey, man. We're gonna look out for you in minute, a'ight?" Nigel says as Chase unlocks his car door with the remote.

I walk over to Nigel's car parked a few spots down from Chase's and open the passenger's door.

"A'ight, man. In a minute." Chase and I make eye contact and I mouth, "I'm sorry" to my best friend. I hate it when he's mad at me, which quite honestly I think this is the first time it's ever happened. He takes a deep breath in and then lets it out before pulling off.

"Let's get it," Nigel says, starting his engine. "What's up with your boy tonight, Jayd? Looks like he's upset about something."

Carefully considering my words, I answer Nigel in the most honest way that I can. "He's got a lot on his mind."

"No shit." Nigel turns up the volume on the Damian Marley song blaring through the speakers and rolls down the windows. "Don't we all."

His phone rings and he cuts off the music. "What up, man?" Nigel answers through the car speakers.

When I get some funds I'm definitely going to get a hands-free sound system in my car. With the hours I'm working at both shops and my own hustle I should have enough saved up for a car by summer. I know my mom's getting tired of me rolling hers all of the time. And it seems to be a break-in magnet now that I'm the primary driver. Inglewood has always been a hot spot but with me rolling around from hood to hood it just seems like it's becoming a more frequent thing, not to mention my haters making me and anything that's mine a moving target.

"Make a left on Rosecrans, Nigel. Nellie's in trouble, again." Chase says, scaring me.

"What happened?" I ask. Now I know why she was acting so strange a little while ago. "Is Nellie okay?"

"No, she's not. We need to get her to the hospital but she doesn't want to go."

Nigel reaches Nellie and Chase in two minutes. We both jump out of the car at the sight.

"Nellie." I kneel down next to where she's seated on the curb and attempt to touch her bare shoulder but she flinches. I stop short of making contact. She looks like she was in a fight, or worse. "Chase, what happened to her?"

"David," Chase says, gritting his teeth in anger. "She said something about her smiling at Nigel with too much teeth tonight."

"Where's that punk ass fool, Nellie?" Nigel asks, punching his right fist into the palm of his left hand. "I'll make sure that he never smiles with teeth again."

"He's gone," Nellie says, wiping the tears from her cheeks. "I told you, I'm fine. I just want to go home, take a hot shower, and forget this day ever happened."

"We can't do that, Nellie. Come on, let me help you up." Chase reaches for her hand but his ex girlfriend's not having it.

"Get away from me," Nellie says, pushing Chase's hand away. "This is all your fault! If you'd never left me in the first place for that skank, Alia I wouldn't be here. I would have never been..." Nellie's voice trails off into the same lost place as her eyes do.

"You wouldn't have been what, Nellie?" Nigel moves Nellie's chin with his index finger and forces her to focus on him and him alone.

"I wouldn't have been..." she begins, but whatever it is she can't bring herself to say. Again, she drifts off. What did that punk do to her?

"Let's get you to the ER, Nellie." I attempt to help her to her feet but she won't let me.

"Don't touch me!" Nellie screams. "It's just as much your fault as it

110

is his. You took him from me, Jayd. He can never love anyone else because of you." Nellie stumbles to her feet and uses Nigel's forearm as leverage. "You take everything away, you weird bitch! And I know these guys aren't even that into you. You put spells on people, Jayd. Cameron knows all about your little tricks and one day you're going to get what's coming to you. Believe that."

That sounded like a threat. I know she's having a hard night but she's completely lost it if she thinks I'm going to take the blame for her boyfriend's actions. What I need to do is get inside of her head and bypass all of the bull.

"I got this, Jayd," Nigel says, distracting me from my thoughts. "Chase, you two go ahead. I'm going to make sure Nellie get's home safely after I get her checked out."

"Yeah, and I'm sure you'll make sure Jayd gets home safely too, right Chase?" Nellie's acting more like the aggressor than the victim that she is in this scenario. She's always been the jealous kind but I had no idea that she could be a spiteful heffa when she wants to be. I guess bitchiness is a contagious virus and Cameron's the main carrier of the disease.

"Nigel, let me know if you need anything," Chase says, choosing to take the high road and ignore his ex.

I'm glad he spoke up because at the moment I'm tempted to lay into her, damn her current state of mind.

"Will do." Nigel takes off his letterman jacket, wraps it around Nellie's shoulders, and then leads her to his car. She looks tossed like a goddamn salad and wants to come at me all crazy like. What the hell is wrong with her?

"And you wanted to run around telling everyone about us," I say once we're back on our way to Maggie's cousin's house. I'm glad that we're still going to make an appearance, not only to celebrate Maggie's victory, but also because I need to speak to Javier and Mauricio about our master plan.

"Jayd, I understand that you want to protect your friends but I'm your friend too, you know. And I also have your best interest at heart always. Can you really say that about the people you're trying to keep in the dark about us?"

"That's not the point," I say, trying to defend my stance once again. But there's something about his logic that's slowly winning me over.

"I agree that's not the point. I think the real deal is that you really don't want to be with me out and about because you're not sure that you want to be with me at all."

"Chase, that is so far from the truth," I begin, but even I can hear the uncertainty in my statement.

"Really, Jayd? I've known you for too long for you to try and convince me otherwise, girl. Look, I love you, okay?" He momentarily takes his eyes off of the road to look me in the eye. "That's never going to change, so don't start lying to me now. You can always be real with me, Jayd. I hope you know that."

"Of course I know that, Chase. And I love you, too. But you're right. I'm not sure that I want to be with anyone right now. However, I do know that there's no shame in my game when it comes to you and me." Truth be told, I'd be lucky to be his girl. It's just so complicated and I feel like I've been through the ringer lately between Keenan, Jeremy and Rah. Chase is just the kind of peace that I need in my world, but the hurricane that is my life won't allow for a moment calm enough to truly explore all that we could be.

When we arrive at Pete's house there are folks hanging out outside on the sprawling lawn. The driveway's full of pimped-out classic cars and a couple of modern ones are also in the mix. It's a mesa-styled home at the top of a hill with a great view of the Manhattan Beach Pier. I knew her family was big but damn. I had no idea they were also balling out like this.

"Chica!" Maggie screams from the front porch. She and her sister are sitting on one of the two wooden swings enjoying the live deejay right on the other side of the front door. "What took you so long, and where's my prince?"

"Nigel had an emergency to handle," Chase says, kissing Maggie on the cheek.

I give Maggie a hug and she pulls me down in between her and her sister. "Why are you so formal, lady? We're family, no?"

"Si, Maggie. We're family," I say, smelling the alcohol on her breath. I didn't know that she drank but I can't say that I'm surprised. I'm the only one of my friends who doesn't drink, other than Nellie who likes to pretend like she does when around certain company.

"Speaking of family, where are Mauricio and Javier?" Chase asks, looking around. "We need to holler at them."

"Claro que si, papi," Maggie says, taking my hand and pulling me up with her. To be so tiny this chick sure is strong. "They're inside shooting pool or playing dominoes or something else. Boys love their games, especially when there's money involved." Maggie grabs Chase with her free hand and walks us inside.

We step down into the sunken living room that's probably as

large as my mom's entire apartment. This is the ultimate game room. In two corners are card tables where folks are playing poker and from what I can tell spades. The pool table is on the far right side adjacent to the patio doors that lead out onto the deck where there are even more people outside chilling. I love how open the floor plan is. It's the perfect place for entertaining.

"Well, who do we have here?" a very handsome man says looking my way. "Que paso, Chase?"

"This is my girl, Jayd. And Jayd, this is Pete," Maggie says, playfully slapping her cousin's arm. "Recuerdo, I told you about her. She's the reason I won tonight."

"Jayd, of course," Pete says, standing up from the table without relinquishing his hand of cards. "Welcome to my home." He kisses me on my right cheek then my left and reclaims his seat at the poker table.

"Thank you," I say, feeling my cheeks turn red. "You have a lovely home."

"Gracias, Jayd. We built it from the ground up, me and mi familia," Pete says, nodding at the other three men at the table, including Mauricio and Javier.

"It's good to see you again, Jayd," Mauricio says. He and Javier both greet us without rising from the table. I guess it's a serious game, even among family.

"It's nice to meet you as well. I'm Paco, senior cousin to all these putas."

Pete punches Paco in the arm before taking a sip of his beer. "Help yourselves to some food and there's plenty to drink and smoke of course. And Chase, we can take care of that business anytime you're ready, man."

"After we eat," Chase says, eyeing the spread in the adjacent kitchen.

After piling our plates with Mexican food and wings, we take a seat on the couch and watch the intense card game.

"So my cousins here tell me that you're the chick we've been looking for, si?" Pete says without taking his eyes off of his hand.

"I don't know what you mean." This is the best carne asada I have ever tasted, and I've had some tasty Mexican food in my day. His grandmother was in the kitchen making more food like they're going to run out soon.

"Don't be shy, Jayd," Pete says, smiling. "There are no secrets here."

"Pete had a run-in with Esmeralda's guard beast not too long ago," Mauricio says. "If Don Juan wasn't there, mi primo might not have been here to tell the story." Mauricio nods his head at the massive pit bull laid out by the fireplace.

Although Rousseau is a powerful entity, even he has to have the good sense to be afraid of a pit when it's not under his control.

"I'm glad you got away unscathed," I say, taking a sip of my pineapple Jarritos. I might have to go back for another one. There are so many flavors to choose from and I love them all.

"Who says I wasn't hurt?" Pete rolls up his pant leg to display a scratched up right leg. "That's why this shit is long overdue."

"First she messed with our money, now she's coming after us physically," Javier says, puffing on his blunt. "It's time to put the bitch down once and for all, you feel me?" He lays his hand on the table and reveals his full house spread.

"Shit, man," Mauricio says, throwing his cards down. "I knew you were sitting on something but I didn't know it was like that."

"I guess it's just my lucky night." Javier claims the chips in the center of the table while Mauricio retrieves all of the cards to reshuffle.

"So how do you propose we stop Esmeralda in her tracks?" Pete asks.

"Well, I've already started the process," I say without revealing too much information.

I'm not sure how much Maggie told them about how I get down and she's nowhere to be found at the moment. I have a feeling her and her boyfriend are somewhere celebrating her win in their own special way.

"Is that right?" Pete says, suspiciously. "What do you need us for, then? Seems like you've got everything under control, unless there's something you're not telling us?"

"Something like what?" I say, getting defensive. Who the hell does he think he is questioning my motives? His family came to me, need I remind him.

"I don't know," he says, puffing on the blunt. "You know it's a tricky world out here, mija. The people who should have your back are usually the first ones to stab you in it, you feel me?"

"Yes, I feel you but not your insinuation."

"Pete, Jayd's cool, man," Chase says, accepting the blunt. "She's with me."

"Yeah, I see that, Chase. And you and me, we've been partners for a long time, si? Never have you ever brought a girl up in my space, and then when you do she just so happens to be the neighbor to a bruja I want out of business. Not to mention, from what mi prima says, Jayd is a bruja herself, no?"

Mauricio and Javier are silent but I can tell they want to jump to my defense. There must be some sort of seniority code I don't know anything about. And Paco doesn't appear to care one way or another, as long as no one touches his tacos, his beer, or his cards.

"I'm not a witch and I resent the implication that I'm anything like Esmeralda," I say, coming to my own defense.

"But aren't you two sides of the same coin? How do I know that she didn't put you under her influence, papi?" Pete says to Chase sounding a bit like Nellie. "Huh? How do I know that she's not holding you by the huevos and controlling your wallet at the same time? Like I said, the first chick I've ever seen you with. Can't be a coincidence. I just don't believe in them."

"Pete, man. You're wrong about Jayd," Javier says, finally speaking up.

Mauricio nods in agreement. "She's on our side."

"How do you know anything about this girl, Javier? She could be manipulating all of you just like that cold bitch with her evil eyes and shit. Gives me the creeps just thinking about her."

Pete must've had more than one run-in with Esmeralda to fear her this much.

"Are you afraid of her?" I ask him point-blank. These dudes may be afraid of him but I could give a damn about angering Pete. He can't insult my lineage without retribution.

"Yes, and you should be too. Unless, like I said, you're working with her."

"I'm not afraid of her because me and my grandmother have beat her at her own twisted games more than once," I say, placing my empty soda bottle down on the floor. "And I will always win because that's who I am."

"And who are you, again? You never did say exactly what it is that you did to her, and what you want me, us, to do for you." Pete lights another cigar and looks at me as if he's already won this game he's playing with me.

"My name is Jayd, Jayd Jackson. And I am the youngest in a long, long line of voodoo priestesses who have been taking down people like Esmeralda for a very long time."

"Si, I know you are a Santera, or a wannabe one at least. Tu abuela though, she is the real thing. I know of Queen Jayd, also known as Lynn Mae." At least he has some respect for my grandmother. "But you, little Jayd, I just don't know about. How do I know you don't want to be in the weed game, mami? How do I know that you're not working with that punk ass bitch, G and his puta, Mickey?"

Chase looks at me and I at him. What isn't he telling me?

"Mickey and I are friends, that's true. But I hate her man almost as much as I hate Esmeralda."

"I don't know, mija," Pete says, shaking the sweet smelling cigar in my direction. "There are just too many coincidences with you."

"Maybe that's a good thing," Chase says, intervening. He knows that I'm about to go off. "Jayd's on the inside in more ways than one. Isn't that what you need to get back what Esmeralda stole from you, from us?"

See, now I know he's not telling me everything. "I don't need this shit," I say, putting my half-eaten plate down on the coffee table in front of us, ready to leave. "If you want my help you know where to find me. either way, I will get back at Esmeralda with or without y'all. Thanks for the late dinner."

"Wait a minute, Jayd," Pete says, smiling. "You're a fiery one, no? Don't take it personally, mija. I have to make sure that you're not trying to take on more than you can handle, including what rightfully belongs to us."

"Look, all I want is total control over Esmeralda's zoo so that I can free Misty, Emilio, and whoever else's spirit she's got trapped inside of that house of hers." I look at Pete who is still unconvinced of my true motives. "Would you tell him, please?" I say to Javier and Mauricio. "I don't want your money, your contraband, or anything else that you think you have to offer me. I just want inside of that house. Whatever else you find is on you."

"Okay, okay," Pete says, putting his hands up in mock surrender. "You win, mija. We will help you get what you need. And like you said, whatever else we find is definitely on us."

"Then it's settled," Chase says, rubbing my shoulders. This is one time I'm glad to be claimed by him. "Let us know when it's going down. We'll be ready."

"Forgive me," Pete says, gesturing around toward the kitchen. "Let's start over again. Me llamo Pete. Welcome to mi casa. Eat, drink, be merry and all of that good shit. Tonight we celebrate. Tomorrow we plot against our common enemy."

Sounds good to me. In the meantime I'll just breathe and enjoy the rest of the night and worry about the rest tomorrow.

"What happens between me and Mickey is between me and Mickey."
-Nigel
Drama High, volume 7: Hustlin'

~ 9 ~
# WOO SAA

"Jayd, I'm so glad you could make it, girl," Rah says, kissing me on the cheek. "How was your flight?"

"It was good, as usual," I say, taking a seat in the chair he's pulled out for me. I set my briefcase and purse down on the cloth-covered chair to my left and make myself comfortable at the intimate table. "Any flight that takes off and lands safely is a good flight to me."

"I know that's right." Rah sits down across from me and hands me a menu. "It's good to see you. You're looking good, as always."

The platinum and diamond band on his left ring finger is still as stunning as ever, although time has dulled it a bit. "How's your family?"

"The girls are good," he says, eyeing the menu. "And my son just started walking. He's terrorizing the house, the dog, and anything else he can get his hands on."

"That's great, Rah. I'm glad everything's going well for you." I've decided on the shrimp and crab bisque. He always picks the wine.

The waiter comes to take our order and delivers warm bread and water with lemon—just how I like it.

"How's everything with you?" he asks, taking a sip of his water. Rah doesn't eat carbs anymore. He says it interferes with his fitness regimen. As a Major in the Army he always has to be in top shape to set a prime example for his unit and his family.

"All is well," I say, taking a bite of my buttered rye. "I should make partner in my firm by the end of the year. Hell, as much as they have me travelling lately I should've been partner a long time ago."

"Well you must be their most important attorney if they're sending you to represent their biggest clients all over the world." Rah pours the high-end Pinot into my glass first and then his. "Cheers to a powerful and beautiful soon-to-be partner."

"Thank you." After all of these years he can still make me blush. "I don't know how powerful I am, and these days I don't feel so beautiful." If I could I'd open the top button on my pants that are a bit too snug before my meal, and I'd take off my bra. The forty pounds I've put on since finishing law school don't suit me very well.

"Stop it, girl," Rah says, his eyes piercing into my soul. "You're beautiful and you always will be to me."

"Rah, please don't," I plead. "You have a family and I'm unavailable."

"Oh, I didn't know you were seeing anyone," he says, taking a large swig of the expensive wine. "My apologies."

"I'm not, but my work is the only spouse I have time for." I match his gulp and we sit in an awkward silence for a few moments.

"As usual." Rah refills both of our glasses and we resume our drinking.

Things are usually easy and pleasant between us when I can make it back to LA for business or to visit my family, but there's always an undertone of what could have been. Once he married Trish I left LA and attended Harvard for law school. With all of the pain that I left behind I never even thought about moving back home.

"Rah, why do you always check on me? Why do you insist on us seeing each other every time I come to Los Angeles when you and I both know that there's nothing here for us anymore?" We've gone in and out of our long lasting love affair but haven't been with each other in years. Once I realized that he'd never leave Trish for too long I stopped that bull and regained my self-respect. But yet and still I always find myself obliged to break bread with the brotha when possible.

"We're going to know each other forever, Jayd. You do know that, don't you? No matter what, no matter who else is in the picture, you'll *always know me and I'll always know you. Forever," he says, raising his third glass. "Death can't even do us part."*

"Isn't that the same oath you took with your wife?" I claim my wine glass and finish off the contents without meeting his.

"Yes it is but I took the same oath with you first, remember?" he says, joining me in drinking without toasting. "I know you're not a practicing priestess anymore since your grandmother passed away, but tell me that you don't still enjoy our occasional dreams?"

Mama's death is still a sensitive subject no matter how long it's been since her passing. However, just like I can communicate with her although she's transitioned to the ancestor realm, Rah and I continue to share dreams occasionally, which is why I can't maintain a relationship with anyone else for too long. What man wants to hear his woman scream another man's name on a regular basis?

"Rah," I begin, but anything I say in objection would be a lie.

"They are sweet, aren't they?"

He moves into the empty seat to my right and reaches underneath the thick tablecloth where he finds my left thigh. His mere touch excites me more than any other man's ever could. Rah rubs my leg and slowly progress upward, exciting me more with every stroke.

"Not here. Not now," I mutter. "Please, Rah. We can't."

"Why can't we, Jayd? It's just us. It's always going to be just us in here, forever." Rah continues his exploring and I surrender to the good feeling. It's been too long since a man has touched me the way that he's doing right now.

"Rah," I sigh. The alcohol relinquishes any ounce of decorum left in my limp body. How does he know exactly what buttons to push and when?

"I'm here, Jayd," he whispers. *"And I'm not going anywhere. Not ever. Just breathe, baby. I've got you."*

"I know you do, Rah," I moan. *"I know you do."*

The alarm rings on my phone and wakes me up from yet another shared dream between Rah and me. What. The. Hell! I've got to get a handle on this shit before I wake up to Chase staring at my guilty ass. I know there are no jade bracelets to represent my first love but there's got to be a way to keep him from entering my subconscious mind at-will. Yet another issue for me to work on, I suppose.

My entire Sunday morning was spent at Simply Wholesome. I don't know why I've put all of this extra weight on my plate, especially while plotting Esmeralda's demise with Sin Piedad to help. Do I really want to go through with this apprenticeship? What will this do for me, and is there another way to go about it without sacrificing my joy and what little free time have? There has to be another way to get the money I need to pay my mom's insurance company because this shit ain't working. Anything that hampers my flow is bad for my health and that can't be the right way to go. Something's got to give and it's not going to be my sanity again.

My mom's fiancé let me borrow his extra car that my mom's been rolling in since they met so that I could get back and forth today. All I had to do was get to my mom's crib from Chase's house. It's times like these that I'm glad I held on to my bus pass. Chase was knocked out from last night's adventures when I left this morning and is probably still asleep. I have to drop the car back off at my mom's apartment in a little while but wanted to drop by and check on Nigel. He texted us last night after he got Nellie home safely. Even with winning the game and being crowned a prince he was understandably done for the night after that.

I pull up in front of Nigel's house and join the line of parked fancy cars. Actually, Karl's Camry is the newest out of them all but that doesn't matter. Age isn't the main factor when comparing cars. In somebody's eyes a car will be the shit as long as it has tinted windows, rims, and a booming sound system. I park behind Nigel's Impala, which is parked next to Mickey's car. What the hell kind of crap am I about to step into this afternoon?

"Hi, Mrs. Esop," I say as I approach the front door. I can't believe my eyes but I know they're not playing tricks on me this time. She's holding a peaceful Nickey who smiles at me as if to say, "See, I told you that I'm supposed to be right here." This little baby is more than a handful.

"Jayd, so nice of you to join us," Mrs. Esop says. She and Nickey are outside enjoying the sunshine. "I think this year is going to be the best year ever for my roses, don't you think so?"

"They're beautiful as usual, Mrs. Esop." Nickey smiles as I tickle her belly and kiss her hands. "How's everything going?"

"Everything's as well as can be expected," she says, shifting Nickey from the front of her tall body to her right hip. "I've missed holding a baby. They bring such peace to a household, don't you agree?"

"Yes, they do have their own calming energy, I suppose." I try to catch Nickey's eyes so that I can see what's really going on for myself before I step inside, but Mrs. Esop keeps moving around the garden and blocking my view.

"Your friends are inside talking with our attorney. I think that girl has finally come to her senses about this unfortunate ordeal." Ms. Esop gives a slight smile and I know that she thinks she's won this battle.

I do feel sorry for her, especially since both of her children have pretty much banned her from their personal lives because of her overbearing ways. And I'm quite sure that Mrs. Esop would make the perfect substitute mother for Nickey if it were ever truly necessary, but taking a child that has no blood relation to her away from the mother is a low down dirty shame. I hope that Mickey hasn't done something out of fear that can't be easily undone. I'd better get inside and check the situation out for myself.

"What up, girl?" Nigel asks, only taking his eyes off his PS4 game for a moment to greet me. "How was the party?"

"It was cool," I say, sparing him the details of me negotiating with Maggie's relatives about how to get away with murdering Esmeralda's plans for a global voodoo takeover. "The food was excellent, so that's all that really matters."

"That's what's up." Nigel expertly maneuvers the controls as Laura Croft evades death time and time again. If my life were only that easy.

"I saw your mother with Nickey outside," I say, looking around the living room. "Where's Mickey?"

"She's in my dad's office with my parents' attorney," he says, nodding his head toward the closed door. "I guess she's got to sign some papers or some shit. I don't know."

I take a seat on the couch next to Nigel and consider walking over to the office door but I can't offer any more advice to Mickey. She should've listened to me and asked Chase's mom to represent her, or at least offer her some expert counseling pro bono, but Mickey just has to be difficult even when it comes to something as serious as keeping custody of her child.

"How's Nellie?"

"She was okay when I called and checked on her earlier today," Nigel says, finally making eye contact with me for more than a quick moment. "I told her to go get checked out but she said it wasn't necessary."

"From what I saw last night I disagree," I say, shaking my head at her situation. "How did she get herself into an abusive relationship with that punk ass fool in the first place?"

"I don't know but I have an idea about how to get her out of it once and for all." Nigel presses the game controller keys hard like he's trying to teach them a lesson.

131

Laura Croft jumps off of a building, rolls onto the snow-covered ground and points her gun out in front of her. A man comes out from behind a wall and she shoots him-point blank in the head. Nigel moves the controller's keys so that Laura is now standing over another unfortunate soul. He has her point the gun at his head and shoots him right between the eyes.

"Damn, Nigel. I saw the movie but had no idea the game was this violent."

"That's life, ain't it though?" Nigel says, without taking his eyes off of the carnage that he's creating. "One minute I'm playing the game of my life and leading my team to our second homecoming win in a row, the next I'm picking up a friend who's been beat up by some chump-ass nigga."

"That's why you have to stop and breathe, Nigel." I say, touching his hand. I pull my hand away from what I feel. "What the hell happened to your knuckles?"

"Oh, that's from the game, girl. What do you think we're out there doing, crocheting?"

"Nigel I was with you last night, remember?" I feel his hands again and this time he's the one who flinches. "And your knuckles were not beat up after the game." And then it dawns on me. He was in a fight, but with who?

"Jayd, just drop it, okay?" Nigel says, looking me in the eye. "Like I said, I hurt my fist playing ball last night. Nothing else happened, okay?"

"If you say so, Nigel." Before either one of us can contest any further, the office door opens and Mickey comes out looking like she's been crying for hours.

"Hey, Mickey," I say, walking over to her. "What was that all about?"

"It was about this little punk right here trying to get me locked up if I don't agree to his visitation terms," Mickey says, almost spitting she's so upset. "How could you do that shit to me, Nigel, and claim to love my daughter? My daughter!" she screams at the top of her lungs.

Nigel doesn't budge. "Like I said before, she's my daughter too. Whatever you decide to do with your life is your business, but I'll be damned if you ruin Nickey's life in the process."

"You've got some serious nerve trying to tell me what to do, Nigel."

"Oh, and make sure you keep that criminal away from my baby or you know what'll happen next."

"You'll get what's coming to you, Nigel. Trust me, this ain't over. Not yet." Mickey walks over to Nigel and spits in his face.

"Cute, Mickey. Real cute," Nigel says, wiping his face clean with the back of his bruised hand. "See yourself out of my house before I press charges."

"Kiss my black ass, Nigel," Mickey says, making her way to the front door. "All of it."

"Been there. Done that." Nigel laughs at Mickey's anger and continues playing his game.

I guess I'll get going, too. I have to get Karl's car back and I don't want to keep Chase waiting. He texted me a while ago asking if I needed a ride back to his place after work and I said I'd be at my mom's apartment by now. Unfortunately my phone died and the car charger's still in my mom's ride.

Chase was waiting in his car when I pulled into my mom's parking space. I am always packed so he didn't have to wait too long for me to come back downstairs once I locked up my mom's apartment.

"I stopped by Nigel's before coming back here," I say. He's been quiet since I got in and that was twenty minutes ago. "I think something happened last night after we left him with Nellie. He looks like he was the one in a fight."

"I'll check in with him later. By the way, you had an interesting dream last night," Chase says, instantly changing the subject. Did he hear a word I just said?

"What do you mean?" My cheeks are burning with embarrassment. Please tell me that one of my worst fears did not come true.

"You were moaning Rah's name during your dream, Jayd. More than once."

And there it is. "They're just dreams, Chase. I can't control them." That's not exactly true, but this particular one was out of my hands.

"I know that but still. Your subconscious speaks volumes, especially for you."

"Not always," I say, but that's not entirely true either.

"I'm not stupid, Jayd. You know I love you, and I know that you love him," Chase says. "You say his name in your dreams."

I'm speechless. It's one thing to defend my conscious actions, but what I do and say in my dream state is another beast entirely.

"I'm sorry," I say, but Chase isn't feeling me.

"I don't know why I'm not, Jayd. We are friends above all else. And, even though our crew's split up at the moment, Rah's cool with me and probably always will be. But I would be lying if I could honestly say that I thought for a minute you could ever love me like you love him. I may have been your first lover in the flesh but he was the first in your mind, and that right there is what you call the gospel."

"The gospel?"

"Yup. Church; preach." Chase pulls into his driveway and puts the car in park without cutting it off. "I've got to take care of something real quick. I'll be back."

"Chase," I begin, but I can tell he needs some time to calm down. "Be careful."

"Always am." He watches me open the front door and pulls off back down the hill.

I step inside of the empty house and settle in, charging my phone before all else. Before I can sulk in my self-pity for too long my phone vibrates with a call.

"Jayd, what's going on with you, girl?" Keenan asks. It's nice to hear a friendly voice after all of the bull I've been dealing with.

"Oh, nothing much. Just been busy as all get-out," I say, closing the front door behind me. I need to take a walk to clear my head. This is my first argument with my best friend turned lover. Arguments never feel good, but this one has got me all twisted.

"As usual, right?" Keenan's been very patient with me in more ways than one.

"Keenan, I know I lead you on last time we were together..." I begin, but he interjects before I can continue with my apology.

"Girl, please. I'm not worried about that," he says dismissively. "I'm just checking on your ride and wanted to see if you're still game for joining my study group when you have some time to spare. I miss hanging out with you; that's all."

Keenan can be an elitist jerk sometimes but for the most part he's cool to kick it with. Besides, I learn a lot from him every time we're together.

"You know what? I could use the distraction but my mom's car is still not fixed," I say, walking down the steep hill. The sun begins to set in the horizon casting a reddish-orange hue on the gorgeous homes in PV. I for one am glad to see this day come to a close, even if it does mean going to school tomorrow.

"That's what I like to hear," Keenan says. I can hear his smile through the phone.

"What's that?" I ask, smiling in return.

"A yes. I'll call you and let you know what's up. I've got to get back to work, Jayd. Enjoy the rest of your Sunday."

That'll be difficult to do since I have to go back to the same house where I hurt my best friend's feelings without meaning to. I wonder if Chase and I will ever be the same after taking our friendship to the next level. I can't afford to loose any more friends, not real ones. There just aren't that many left in my circle. Besides, there's something very special about Chase, which is why we've been friends since my first day at South Bay High. Whatever I have to do to make sure that at the end of the day me and Chase are still cool is a top priority. I'll be damned if Rah ruins yet another relationship of mine while he rides off into the sunset with his imperfect relationship with Trish in tact. Not this time.

"How come every time a new dude pops up I become second in line?"
-Jayd
Drama High, volume 5: Lady J

~10~
OH HELL NO

When Chase returned last night he told me that Sin Piedad is ready to move forward with my plan, no more questions. I guess I finally checked out enough for Pete's approval, that or something else happened that I'm not yet aware of. Whatever the case, I'm glad that they're finally on board with following my lead. Now if only I could get Chase to be as agreeable. After he filled me in he went into the game room and watched movies by himself for the rest of the night.

Nigel's also been in a peculiar mood. He and Mickey have been giving each other evil looks all morning with neither of them blowing up. Whatever his attorney said to her yesterday put her ass in check and then some. But I can tell that there's another reason Nigel's been preoccupied. I'm pretty sure it has something to do with his battered hands. Every time I try to get a confession out of him he changes the subject. In a minute I'm going to skip asking and just take the answer from him.

"Hi Nigel," Nellie says, a bit to perky for someone who just went through what she did a couple of days ago. "I bought you a little thank you gift, you know, for coming to my rescue the other night."

"Nellie, that's not necessary," Nigel says, slightly embarrassed. "We're friends, right?"

"Right," she says, looking slightly disappointed. She's always had it bad for Nigel but he didn't look at any other girl twice once he met Mickey last year. "But still, you deserve something special for going out of your way even if I am just a friend as you say."

Nigel opens the box to reveal an antique pocket watch. Well damn. She never bought Chase anything like that when they were together.

"My father collects them. I bought it at the same place my mom and I purchase his from. Do you like it?"

"It's very nice, Nellie." Nigel lifts the watch up by it's chain and admires the craftsmanship.

Nellie's face lights up with pleasure. Oh, hell no. This broad is not seriously gunning for Mickey's ex-man and baby-daddy. That is a serious violation, I don't care how messed up their friendship is at the moment. Nellie's just asking for more drama than she can handle from Mickey.

"I knew you'd love it," Nellie says, touching the silver chain. "It's classy, just like you."

Nigel looks at Nellie and realizes that this is more than a simple thank you gift. From the look of it, he doesn't want more of Mickey's drama either. "Nellie, seriously, this is too much. I can't accept it." His mouth says to give it back but his eyes are not letting the bling go so easily.

"I won't hear it," she says, putting her hands over his and forcing a tighter grip on the watch. "It's yours and besides, I can't return it. See you at lunch?"

"Yeah; okay." Nigel looks at me as if to say, "What am I going to do?"

I don't know what to tell the brother.

"Later." Nellie practically skips down the main hall toward her third period class.

I'm glad to see her happy again but damn, she's going to fall hard when she realizes that Nigel's just the kind of dude who'll rescue a friend in need—any friend. He and Rah are chivalrous like that. And so is Chase, if she didn't notice, who was also there trying to help her Saturday night. So was I for that matter.

"Jayd, did you know about this?" Nigel says, putting the box in his backpack.

"Oh no," I say, shaking my head in testimony. I can't help but smile at my boy's obvious astonishment. He's not used to Nellie's ways. "I'm just as surprised as you are, sir."

We head down the main hall in the opposite direction. ASB drones are busy removing the homecoming evidence while at the same time putting up posters about the Halloween dance in a couple of weeks. They're also posting more reminders to purchase our senior rings and yearbook packages while they're still on sale at a discounted price.

"Maybe you can pawn it to help pay for my senior package," I say, attempting to get a chuckle out of Nigel but he's too stuck in his own head to laugh at my jokes.

"Jayd, I'm serious. I don't want to hurt the girl's feelings. She's already been through so much. But still, I can't accept gifts from her when I know she's feeling me like that."

"You're just going to have to set her straight before she buys y'all matching rings and monogramed hand towels and shit." I nudge his arm with my shoulder.

Nigel's not amused. "Jayd, seriously. You have to talk to your girl and make sure she's thinking straight."

"Ha!" I say, attempting to control my laughter. "First of all, Nellie never thinks straight. And second of all, in case you haven't noticed, she's not exactly heeding my advice these days. Shit, she's barely my girl. You're on your own this time, dude."

We walk through the double-doors leading to the courtyard with a couple of minutes remaining to make it to fourth period on time. The further down we walk the more we notice a crowd gathered near the senior quad. We can't help but to join the nosy onlookers. I hope it's not a fight and if it is, I hope it's not one of my friends involved. It shouldn't be because of the protection that the crème puffs should provide us from our enemies.

"Oh, hell no," Nigel says. His height gives him an advantage I don't have to see over the crowd.

"What happened?" I ask, tugging on Nigel's jacket sleeve like a toddler.

Nigel looks down at me and carefully considers his words before answering. "It's Jeremy. He's been busted by the Narcs, again."

The last time this happened was the first time that I went rogue and baked some sweets to get him out of going to jail. What has he gotten himself into now?

"Damn it," I say, pissed that my wish of it not being a friend of mine went completely ignored. "How bad is it?"

Nigel looks through the crowd and reports back. "Pretty bad. They've got evidence and he's handcuffed. It looks like he's going down for this one, Jayd."

"Why didn't it last longer?" I ask out loud.

Nigel looks at me confused at first, and then he recognizes. "I don't know, but whatever you did you need to ask for an extension." Nigel's right. While I'm working on executing my revenge with Sin Piedad I have to figure out what went wrong with my protection recipe.

"I'm telling you, I was set up," I hear Jeremy plead. "I wouldn't be stupid enough to bring anything on campus when I'm on probation. Think about it." His words go unheard by the narcotics officers who rapidly escort him toward the main office.

As they cross the packed courtyard Jeremy passes directly in front of me and I'm finally able to see his face for myself.

"I didn't do this. I swear." I know he's speaking in general but my sight locks onto his and it's as if his speaking to me and only me.

The events of the morning replay in front of me like a recorded television show on fast-forward. Jeremy was checked out by the narcs after Cameron left an anonymous tip during the break as payback for him giving me the iPod. Really, Cameron? She still hasn't learned that I am not to be trifled with but she's about to find out. Just like for Esmeralda, I have something for her ass, too.

Our eyes unlock as Jeremy's forced through the double-doors and the bell rings, indicating that we're all late for class.

"I have to go, Nigel," I say, hugging my friend who's still tripping off of the watch, and now Jeremy's detainment.

"I'll catch up with you after fourth period, Jayd. We have to help our boy get through this."

"Indeed," I agree. Our crew has damn-near been completely dismantled. The last stones would be me and Chase, and Nigel and Nellie together as couples. That can't happen, especially now that I know that my enemies are out for blood at all cost, goddamn vampires.

As soon as I'm settled in class I request a bathroom pass to see if I can catch Ms. Toni. Lately she and Mr. Cho have been spending every break together that they can get, and with homecoming she was overwhelmingly busy with her ASB duties. Naturally, Ms. Toni isn't in her office at the moment. I'll have to catch up with her another time.

My math teacher wasn't too keen on letting me out of class after I was tardy. I'm sure he regrets letting me slide but no take backs. If he marked me late after the fact he'd have to mark several more students who were also late because of the excitement.

I look toward the main office and catch a glimpse of Jeremy standing in front of the Principal's office awaiting his fate. There's got to be a way to help him out of this mess. It's me that Cameron hates, not Jeremy. Why doesn't the broad just come for me instead of playing games?

"You really didn't think that little batch of nasty-ass biscuits would wield its power over our house for long, did you?" Misty says from behind me, also eyeing Cameron's handiwork, or am I giving Jeremy's faux wifey too much credit?

"You did this to Jeremy?" I ask. Misty caught me off guard with this move. "Didn't you torture him enough last year?"

"Enough?" Misty lets out a laugh that closely resembles a howl too much like Rousseau's for my comfort. "What does this mean, Jayd? When is enough ever enough?" She again twists her blood-red lips into a sadistic grin.

"He did nothing to you, Misty. And for the record, he did nothing to Cameron. She's the one who should be going down for all of the evil she's been up to lately with your help, of course."

"Of course," Misty says, stepping her pointy-toed high-heeled boots closer to me. "Do you think we'd actually let you get away with stealing from her house? Oh no, my dear. That's a crime for which the

146

penalty must be paid in full." Misty's transformation from teen vixen to snake takes place before my eyes instantaneously, scaring the hell out of me.

"Oh shit!" I scream in the middle of the vast hall. Where is Ms. Toni when I need her?

"Don't worry, my pretty. This will only hurt a tiny bit." Misty slithers onto the floor and quickly makes her way to the wall. She masterfully glides up and crosses the bathroom door to block my escape. What the hell?

"Misty, you're not thinking clearly," I say, trying to reason with the cold-blooded creature. "This is isn't you. Esmeralda's just using you to get to me and my grandmother. Once she's done what do you think will happen to you and Emilio? She'll throw you out like yesterday's trash or keep you locked up as one of her pets for the rest of your lives. Is that what you really want?"

"Want? What I really want is for you to suffer like I've suffered, like Cameron's suffering, like Nellie's going to suffer when she finds out about you and Chase playing house," she hisses at me. "Rah and Jeremy just weren't enough for you, Jayd. And I guess that college dude wasn't amused by your weird ways for very long, either."

How does she know so much about what's going on in my world?

147

"Poor Jayd," Misty says, angling her slender form into a striking position. "You still think you're the only one with the power to get inside of other people's thoughts even when you don't want them to? Well, don't you worry about that anymore, sweetie. My godmother's taken care of that little problem for you. You can thank her yourself later."

She further angles her body into the perfect attack pose. There's no way that I can escape the venomous creature that she's become. All I can do is try to control her thoughts but it's no use. Misty's beady black eyes aren't getting caught up in my tricks today.

"Misty, don't do this. Think about the repercussions when my grandmother finds out about you biting me."

"That's exactly what I'm counting on, Jayd. Damn you're slow. And I thought you were the smart one in your sorry crew." Prominently displaying her fangs in the safety of the empty hall, she moves in for the kill. I have no book bag or purse to throw at her creepy ass and there's nowhere to run or hide. All I can do is wish that by some miracle her aim is off and it gives me the chance to escape.

This time my wish comes true. The bathroom door flies open, smashing Misty to the ground where she instantly morphs back into her human form.

"Marcia!" I scream, embracing my new best friend. "Thank you."

148

"Jayd, what's wrong?" she asks, oblivious to the horrible deed she just thwarted. "And what happened to you?" Marcia let's go of me to help Misty up off the floor who's anything but grateful.

"You happened to me," Misty growls. "Another one of your friends?" Misty's manufactured blue eyes glare at me ice cold just like her new blood.

"She's new, Misty," I say, trying to protect Marcia from being next on their hit list. "She's just an associate."

Marcia's eyes drop at the demoted classification but I'll have to explain it to her another time. If Misty thinks that we're any closer than that she'll have her ass for lunch.

"Well, tell your associate to watch her step before she's next in line."

"If anyone needs to watch where they're going it's you and your god family, Misty," I say, undeterred by her threats. "And by the way, they were crème puffs, not biscuits. Get it straight."

"Next time you won't have a clumsy savior, Jayd," Misty says, eyeing Marcia and then focusing back on me. "See you in your dreams." Misty disappears through the doors.

Now I can catch my breath. Usually Misty's words don't faze me too much, but something about that parting statement gives me the chills. What does she know about my dreams?

"What was that all about?" Marcia asks.

"Years of hate, which is why I said what I said about you not really being my friend. Trust me, it would've done you more harm than good to tell her the truth."

"It's okay. I'm not offended," she says, defensively. "Besides, I won't be here long enough to make any real friends anyway, so no worries."

"I do consider you a friend, Marcia," I say, touching her shoulder. She smiles and I know that she believes me. She has to. Pretty soon Marcia may be the only chick that I have on deck.

"I'd better get to class," Marcia says, displaying her hall pass. "See you at lunch?"

"Okay," I say, slowly heading back to class myself.

I think I may have figured out how Misty's up to date on all things Jayd Jackson. More importantly, I think I've figured out a way to throw a monkey wrench into Esmeralda's master plan. I need to let Misty or one or her many other wretched pets take a bite out of me after I taint my blood, which will ultimately ruin their plans. For this, I know I'm going to need to keep Mama in the dark. If she knows that I'm going to put myself in the line of fire for the sake of our lineage she'll stop me from

150

even thinking about it—literally.

"Here comes your broad, KJ, and she doesn't look like she wants to conversate with anybody."
-Nellie
Drama High, volume one: The Fight

~11~
RING THE ALARM

After Misty's metamorphosis and Jeremy's takedown this morning I decided that it was time to move our plan into high gear. Chase and I are not in the best of places but thankfully I can always depend on him to handle business, just like Maggie. I sent out a mass text letting all involved parties know that shit was going today after school and to alert all of the soldiers. Luckily Sin Piedad's ground zero isn't far from school and we've been here plotting together ever since.

"So you mean to tell me that Misty, that cute little morena that you used to hang with, can change from a girl to a snake?" Mario says in disbelief. He's late to the party. "Esta loco, chica. I don't believe it."

"Jayd doesn't lie," Maggie says, having my back while rubbing her man's shoulders. "If she says that puta turned into a queen cobra right in front of her, then I believe her."

"It was actually a rattlesnake, but that's not really important." I smile at Maggie and she returns the gesture.

"You see, that's what I'm talking about," Pete says, puffing on what must be his fifth cigar of the evening. We've been here since the early afternoon and he hasn't stopped smoking yet. "That's why her house has to be stopped, family. We have to go hard."

"I agree," Mauricio says, petting his pit bull who's asleep on the couch next to him. "We have to make sure no one else is hurt by the witch. She's playing on a whole other level that our people in the streets can't defend themselves against. It's not a fair battle."

"Battle?" Javier says, chiming in. "This ain't no battle. This is all out war." He takes his gun out of the holster on his hip and places it on the coffee table. "And I'm shooting to kill this time."

"Hey man," Chase says, pointing at the piece. "Put that away before it goes off by accident."

"I'm just saying," Javier says, reclaiming the gun. "Esmeralda won't get a chance to bite me or anyone else if I have a say so." He replaces the gun by his side and relaxes his stance.

"I feel you, Javier," Maggie says, winking at me. I guess she can tell that I'm a bit uncomfortable with the way this conversation's going. "But let's just see how it goes down before we start planning her funeral, si?"

I just want to stop the bitch in her tracks, and possibly rob her of her powers but these dudes are talking about murder and I'm not down with that. Self-defense, yes. Womanslaughter, no.

153

"Si," Pete agrees. "But we are prepared for the worst case scenario. Now, the plan is to plant your boy here with a fixed sack to carry." Pete looks at Chase who nods his head in agreement. I don't want him to be the mule but because he's tight with me, and I'm sure that Misty and Emilio have already conveyed that information to their godmother, Esmeralda will be more inclined to take advantage of the situation.

"And I'm going to get inside with Jayd's site on my side," Chase says, looking at me with all of the faith in the world.

I have to be on my spiritual Ps and Qs to make sure Chase stays protected. I'd never forgive myself if something happened to him.

"Verdad," Mauricio says. "And then we go for the jugular," he says, making a stabbing motion with his bottle.

"Chase, are you sure about this?" I ask. I touch his knee to connect with him. He's been distant all day long and I know he's feeling a way about me and my uncontrollable dreams. I hope he's not doing this to prove something to me or anyone else. "We can figure out another way."

"There is no other way inside, Jayd. She's been brainwashing niggas for who knows how long into doing her evil deeds. So yes, I'm sure."

"And taking our profits," Pete reiterates, keeping things in perspective for him and his family. "Don't forget that shit."

"Which is completely unforgivable." Javier touches the piece on his side again and I can tell he's envisioning pulling the trigger. "She's taking money out of our kids mouths, mija. We can't let that shit slide or we'll have enemies coming at us from all sides."

"One thing we're not is weak, and she's going to learn not to mess with our territory, her and her allies," Pete says, putting out the cigar butt. "We'll take down Hector next. Right now, it's all about Esmeralda."

"I agree," I say. A female perspective is definitely needed in this male-dominated conversation. "And I think you need to ask your Santero for assistance. We're going to need Ogun, the warriors, and every other orisha and ancestor on our side to be successful in this endeavor."

"Done and done." Pete types a short text and tosses his phone back onto the table. "You handle your ancestors and we'll handle ours. I'm sure they'll see eye to eye on this, mija. Don't you worry your pretty little head about it."

They're grandmother, the very same abuela who made Maggie's homecoming gown and the slamming food at her celebration party, emerges from the hallway quiet as a ghost holding two candles; one black and one green. Without saying a word she places the candles on the mantle above the fireplace and lights them both.

"Ache," Maggie and her cousins say. They each make a cross from their foreheads to their chests and then shoulder to shoulder before kissing their fingers. Their grandmother disappears into the back of the house just as quietly as she appeared.

Chase looks at me and whispers, "What just happened here?"

I smile and whisper, "Later." I know a lot of this stuff is over his head and that's okay. I'll catch him up to speed when we're alone.

"I think we're done here," Pete says. His pregnant wife and two small children walk into the living room through the front door and greet us all. "Jayd, you let me know if you need anything else. Otherwise, we'll see you this weekend to get busy, si?"

"Si," I say, shaking his hand to solidify the arrangement. "And thank you. I don't know what I'd do without y'all."

"No, la reina. Thank you." Mauricio hugs me, followed by Javier. "And no worries. Our boy Chase here is the perfect man for the job."

"Yes, he is." I hug my friend hoping to dispel the tension between us. Some of it's faded away but not all of it.

I'll find a way to make it up to Chase. I know how disconcerting it must've been to hear me moan Rah's name in my sleep. I know I wouldn't be too keen on hearing him moan Nellie or Alia's name after we'd just spent the night together, so I get it. I really do.

"It's settled then," Chase says, pulling away from me. "We all know where we stand to get the job done."

"So, let's do it." Maggie puts her arm around me and I rest my head on her shoulder. At least one of my friends still loves me.

Hopefully once I take care of business my friends will return back to normal. There's nothing wrong with playing solitaire, but I prefer to have my full crew in tact when I face the world. Besides, it's our senior year. We should be enjoying it, not worried about an evil bitch out for blood. However, now that I know how to stop Esmeralda, I'll give her all the blood she wants. Her greed will lead to her ultimate demise and I'll be there to watch it all go down with a front row seat.

When Chase and I got back to his house last night after the meeting, we ate the dinner his mom prepared for us in silence. Afterwards, I moved to the guest room downstairs and he didn't object. Shit. I even thought about asking Netta for the recipe to the sweet spell she gave to Mama, but that's also a done deal. Mama's back to her normal self today, and our clients—and everyone else—are fully aware of the change. Luckily they're used to how we get down here. Very little

157

surprises our customers.

At least the protection spell we cast for Mama's still working, but unfortunately the honeymoon's over between her and Daddy. Since we were apparently able to permanently throw Esmeralda off of Mama's scent, with the help of the old witchdoctor, Netta took the special pin out of her hair and all of the sweetness right along with it. I bet Daddy wishes it were still in place, not that she's forgotten all of the good that happened over the last two weeks. But whatever love spell was there is all but a distant memory.

"Your mother told me that you started training at Simply Wholesome after all," Mama says, wiping her station down. Her last client had so much dandruff you'd think that she was walking around with her own personal snow cloud over her head.

"Yeah, little Jayd. How's that going?" Netta brings me more hair clips to wash in the basin from her last client as well. We never mix clients' hair supplies, which sometimes makes my job a little harder. When in the line of work we're in each client's entire well-being is literally in our hands, including their spiritual selves.

"It's not, to be honest," I say, admitting how much I've been slacking lately. "With all that I've got going on at school I just haven't had time to train like I'm supposed to."

"Supposed to?" Netta says, raising her eyebrow. "Didn't we already have this discussion, child? Who says you're supposed to do a damn thing outside of what you're already doing right now?" Netta takes the Florida water from the top shelf above the sinks and pours a generous amount into the bowl I'm already working in.

"My mom, that's who," I say, remembering the conversation like it was yesterday because she basically repeated herself again when we spoke last night. "She wants me to move my hair braiding business out of her apartment and into a more professional environment, thus the partnership with Shakir via Summer."

"I get so tired of folks telling other people what to do with their talent," Netta says, putting her hands inside of the cool water. "Like you were bothering her by making money."

"That girl is never at home anyway," Mama says, frustrated. "The nerve."

"I can understand that she doesn't want folks all up in her space but I just don't want to work under somebody else doing something that I already know how to do," I say, shuddering at the thought of going in on Friday afternoon instead of coming to the shop. "I don't mean y'all, of course." I smile at my grandmother and godmother, and they both smile at each other and then at me.

159

"Jayd, I'm a great hairdresser, an excellent healer, herbalist, or what ever else folks call me around here," Mama says. "But I am the first to admit that I am an equally horrible employee."

"I know that's right," Netta says, seconding Mama's motion.

"I don't care if it's a job that I love, I hate being under the rule of other people's thoughts." Mama looks into the hand mirror and plays with a wayward strand of silver hair. "Did I ever tell you about this one job I had as a midwife through an organization in New Orleans? Now, I had been doing that type of work for years before I decided to supplement your grandfather's income and work full-time."

"All so they could move out West without being poor when they got here," Netta intervenes. "Travelling is expensive and Los Angeles is one of the most expenses cities to live in. Very different from down South."

"Girl, you want to talk about some privileged heffas, both the clients and my co-workers? Ask Chase's mama, she knows what I'm talking about. They can be some evil and vindictive women when they want to be; even wanted me to wear my head wrapped like my mother had to do back in her day, saying it was more sanitary that way even when the white midwives didn't have to, evil wenches."

"Heffas! All of them," Netta adds. She's always in Mama's corner no matter what.

"And you know that I don't use this word lightly, child, but they were bitches. And I told them all to go straight to hell, except for Chase's mama, of course. She was always kind to me and mine."

And she still is. I know that Mrs. Carmichael senses that something's up between me and her son. As far as I can tell she hasn't taken sides yet. She told me just the other day that I'm the daughter she's never had and always wanted. She reminded me of that this morning when she knocked on my door for breakfast.

"That is why I'll never work for anybody again, save my clients. To hell with a manager or a boss," Netta says. "Or clocking in and out 'cause you got to take a piss. What kind of bull is that?"

"Exactly," I say, in full agreement. "I'm grateful for the opportunity, but Summer wants me to twist and braid like her, only use the products that they sell in the store, and she wants me to be on her schedule and I can't always do that." Not to mention that I'm planning the complete annihilation of our greatest mortal enemy, but they don't need to know about that just yet.

"Then quit," Netta says, as if it's that simple. "Tell her thank you but no thank you and keep it moving, yungin!"

"You don't have to say it quite like that, but I agree with your godmother, Jayd. You've got enough work to do without having to worry about making somebody else's business your own." Mama's right about that. She's always right. It was nice having her so sweet and all, but I much prefer this Mama. She's the truth all day, every day.

"What about my mom?" I ask as I place the rinsed silver clips on a clean, white towel and pass them to Netta.

"What about her?" Mama says.

"Girl, Lynn Marie will be just fine." Netta places, the towel and clips on the long shelf behind the sink. Then she carefully runs her right hand over the clips and spreads them out as she looks at the formation for a moment. This is how she sees what her clients' individual needs are.

"Your mother could learn a thing or two from the way you hustle, Jayd. And I know my daughter. She's probably already planning how she's going to decorate Karl's house after the wedding. I say you negotiate with her about your living space rather than worrying about trying to figure out how you're going to continue to work at a place that you don't want to be."

"Amen, praise the Lord, and Hallelujah to that." Netta says. She is so silly sometimes.

"I must admit that I am a bit worried about what I'm going to do after the wedding this summer."

"Why don't you just stay where you are during the week anyway?" Mama says with more than a little salt in that throw.

"I don't think that's feasible. Besides, this situation is just temporary, Mama."

"Mmmhmmmm, little Miss Fast-Ass," Netta says, bumping my left hip with her right. "Working two jobs, living with a man, and about to tell her boss to go suck it. Sounds like someone's trying to be a grown ass woman to me. You sure there's not something else you want to tell us?" Netta rubs my not-so-flat stomach like there's a baby in there.

"As if!" I say, moving away from her. "Don't even play like that, Netta." That does remind me that I have a doctor's appointment coming up soon. I just want to make sure everything's cool down below and restock my birth control supply. Mickey and Nigel's failed teen parenting experiment is the best birth control ever and Chase is always wrapped up tightly, but I still need to watch my own back in that regard.

"This girl acts like we weren't seventeen once upon a time."

I blush at the thought of them in my shoes.

"Did you ever think that maybe, even after you married Daddy, that you could've had a life with Dr. Whitmore?" I ask. "Maybe he could've been swayed to want what you wanted."

"Part of me wishes that I could've run away with Dr. Whitmore, but that was a sweet, sweet dream, baby," Mama says, sighing deeply.

I guess we all have those types of dreams after all.

"Why didn't you, Mama?" I try to imagine a life where Mama's married to Dr. Whitmore and he became my grandfather and not Daddy. Hell, Mama may have just stopped with my mom and maybe one more kid. A life without my uncles: that would be interesting. "You deserve to be happy."

"Yes I do, and so does he. Like I told you before, he never wanted children and I knew that it was in my destiny to be a mother and a grandmother. How was that going to happen if I ran away with a man who made sure that that part of his chi remained stagnant?"

Damn, I guess she's got a point there, although I'd rather not picture Dr. Whitmore's chi.

"Grown ups have to make grown up decisions, Jayd. And sometimes those decisions suck ass, but they're still the right ones to make."

"Very elegant, Netta." Mama takes out a bag of small, cloth-covered mirrors and spreads them out at her station. "But you're right. Some of the decisions we are forced to make at the many crossroads of life don't make sense in that moment and it may not be what your heart wants, but sometimes your head has to overrule your heart for the greater good."

"Here, little Jayd. Take these to your grandmother." Netta cups my hands and pours several of the dry hair clips into them.

"That's why we all need a little help every now and again taking care of our own heads, Jayd." Mama says a quiet prayer over my hands and then gently shakes them. "Open your hands."

The silver clips fall onto the table mixing with the tiny mirrors. Some are standing straight up while others lie flat. The mirrors are either facing up or down, a lot like when we read the cowrie shells for divinations.

"I told you her head was too hot to sit under a drier," Netta says, peaking over Mama's shoulder. "Next week she'll have a cool mint and aloe vera deep conditioning without the added heat. We don't want to have to bail any of our clients out of jail."

"You're right about that," Mama says, making a note of Netta's recommendations. "Hand me Mrs. Carson's box from the closet, Jayd.

And remind me to call her in the next day or so to move her weekly appointment up. She's about to find out that her husband's still gambling and the shit will hit the fan if I don't give her fair warning."

"How did you get all of that from reading her hair clips, and how do the mirrors help?" I ask as I retrieve the client's box. It's getting late but I have to hear this before I call Chase. He's probably already on his way.

"The best way to tell what's going on in a client's head is to read their clips while washing them. All of their worries and fears can be seen through their hair and scalp issues."

"Seriously?" I knew that Netta could read people through her hairdressing skills but I had no idea that she could go that far with the clips.

"Yes, girl. See, if you'd spend more time apprenticing at the right shop you'd know how to do this by now." Netta starts on another batch of clips and Mama prepares more tiny mirrors to assist.

"The girl's hard-headed, just like her mama was at her age," Mama says, again spreading the mirrors out at her station while awaiting Netta's next batch.

"How do the mirrors help?" I choose to learn with my last few minutes rather than spend my time defending myself. There's no winning with these two as my adversaries.

Mama rolls her eyes at me ignoring her accusation but can't pass up the opportunity to teach. "We use a dressed mirror to help our clients fight off their enemies, and when necessary, to reflect their own evil intentions back on them instead of out into the world."

"Is that right?" I say, amazed at the power of the small reflective tools. This might be exactly what I need to get the job done with Esmeralda.

"Sho nuff," Netta says, passing me the clips to give to Mama.

If I can throw the animals' reflections around and thwart her attacks in the meantime, I should be able to cause just enough chaos in her world to distract her while I snatch her site right out from under her. Chase's special delivery will come with a little something extra in the bag. Because she won't be expecting it, I know she'll open the bag to get her money and deliver her product accordingly. Wait until she takes a cold hard look at her own frightening reflection through the special mirrors. I would say that I don't wish that on my worst enemy but I do, and I hope that she gives herself the worst goddamn headache in the world.

~ 1 2 ~
A TERRIBLE INTIMACY

It's early in the morning, way before dawn. We got the call from Sin Piedad that the exchange was going down at Hector's house before sunrise so we took the initiative to make the move early rather than wait until our planned time. I'm very worried about Chase, especially considering the fact that he's not in the best frame of mind. I put a little extra protection on his bag of goodies as well as the dressed mirrors inside to immediately throw off Hector and Esmeralda. I just hope that they don't figure it out with Chase standing there. Who knows how they'll take it out on him if they figure out that Sin Piedad's working with me.

Chase has been consistent in his wanting to help my cause and for that I'm truly appreciative. But I can't help but wonder if he's having second thoughts since we're still not back to normal.

"Jayd, I'll be fine," he says for the umpteenth time. "I've been here a hundred times before and today's no different."

"I know that, Chase. But it is different today. You usually don't have a spiritual trap hidden within your delivery." I hate to send him

168

into Hector's house without me but we have no other alternative. Sin Piedad's already waiting for us to arrive at our designated spot to escort him the rest of the way.

"I got this, Jayd. Trust me." Chase reaches into the passenger's seat and squeezes my left knee. I've missed his touch.

"Where are we going?" I ask, hoping he got the directions wrong even if this is a regular journey for him.

"What do you mean? Hector lives in San Pedro, just over the bridge."

"I hate bridges," I say, squirming as the light changes from red to green. "How come you didn't tell me about this?" I slide down in my seat, cover my head, and pray.

"I thought you knew about the bridges out here. My badd, Jayd." Chase squeezes tighter as I continue saying my prayers.

Chase pulls over to the side of the road once we make it to the other side of the bridge. He sends a quick text to Javier who turns the corner with Mauricio and Pete also in the truck.

"Okay, remember. Don't look into the bag once you give it to Hector. Be careful, Chase."

"I'll be back, Jayd. Don't worry. Like I said, we got this."

"I know you do." I don't know about the rest of his crew, but I believe in Chase.

After about an hour, Chase and the rest of his crew reemerge looking victorious. "I told you not to worry. Everything went as planned," Chase says, locking the car door behind him.

"And so it begins." I refocus my attention on the bridge behind us as he whips the car around to head for home. We'll still beat the sunrise and hopefully get some more sleep in before the day officially begins. "Do we have to go back over the bridge?" I don't know much about this area but everywhere in LA County has at least two ways in or out.

"It's water, Jayd. There are only two ways to get from here to there. We can go back over the bridge the way we came or catch a boat. Which would you prefer?"

At least I know that he didn't lose his sense of humor no matter how irritated he is with me. "Very funny, Chase."

"Just letting you know you've got options," he says, almost smiling. "It'll be over soon. Just close your eyes and think of something pleasant."

The last time I did that I ended up in another dream with Rah. At some point I guess I'll have to actually call Rah and see if he's remembering the experiences with me. Like crossing the bridge, maybe if I face my fear the mystery will go away, and I'll stop calling out his name in the middle of my dreams.

Once Chase and I got back to his house this morning we both crashed on separate couches in the living room. I think we were both too tired to worry about what I might say in my crazy dreams. Too bad the mutual good sleep was interrupted by frantic calls from both Mickey and Nigel. Just once I'd like to sleep in on a Saturday and not have anywhere to go.

"Jayd, I'm serious. Get your girl before I hurt her," Nigel says through Chase's phone. I don't believe he'd ever lay hands on a girl, but Mickey sure does know how to push all of his buttons.

I've got Mickey on my line and muted my phone so they can't hear each other even if we are all at Nigel's house. We hang up our cells and step inside. Chase can't stay for too long because he promised his mother that he'd accompany her to pay his father an unexpected visit. Hopefully he can still be effective in calming Nigel down in the meantime.

"Mickey, what the hell is going on?" I ask, following her through Nigel's living room.

"Last night Nellie told me that Nigel beat David's ass when he came back for her after homecoming. Knocked his ass out like Mayweather right there on the curb. And the best part is that David's pressing charges against Nigel so we're even, little punk ass."

"Okay, Mickey. You're not thinking clearly," I say, trying to reason with Mickey but she's like a dog with a bone this morning, and she's looking to bury it right into Nigel's back.

"Oh, you are so wrong," Mickey says, climbing the stairs. "Before, I didn't have a chance in hell of fighting their lawyers, but now they don't have a pot to piss in. They'll lose any hope of Nigel securing a football scholarship if this gets out. And if they want me to be quiet now they'll have to do a lot more than leave me and my baby alone for good."

"Mickey, do you really think Mrs. Esop's going to respond favorably to being blackmailed?" Even if Mickey thinks that she's got them right where she wants them, the Esops are quite formidable and not to be toyed with.

Mickey stops at the top of the winding staircase to look me in the eye. "I may not play chess, Jayd, but I know a checkmate when I see one. And from where I'm standing, I'm winning."

"I didn't know that you were coming over, Jayd," Nigel's older sister Natasia says, coming out of the hall bathroom.

172

"Hey, Natasia. That makes two of us," I say, hugging her. "What brings you to Cali?"

"Oh, you know how planning a wedding can be. I had a fitting for my dress and I want to make sure that the bridesmaids are on top of their jobs, too."

"I know both of you are going to be simply stunning." Mrs. Esop still doesn't want to admit that her only daughter's a lesbian, let alone that she's about to marry the love of her life.

"Thanks, Jayd. I'll make sure to add you to the bridal shower invite list." Natasia can no longer ignore a fuming Mickey by my side. They didn't really know each other well when Mickey was dating Nigel, and I'm sure what Natasia knows of her she doesn't care for. "What else is going on?"

"Nigel called me to come and help Mickey out with some paperwork," I say. I'm not sure what Natasia knows about her brother's custody battle and don't want to say too much.

"I see." Natasia and Mickey glare at one another without exchanging fake pleasantries. One thing I can definitely say about Natasia is that she's nothing like her mother in that regard. "Well, enjoy the rest of your day. And don't forget about the shower, Jayd."

173

"I won't." Once Natasia's safely out of earshot I turn to Mickey who hasn't calmed down a bit.

"Can we get on with it now or do you need to finish socializing with the enemy?" Mickey says, charging forward. "Hell, maybe she'll even ask you to be one of her bridesmaids since you're all up in the family like that."

"Mickey, stop," I say, blocking her path in middle of the wide hallway. Nigel's parents' room is at the end and I'm sure the last thing they're expecting to see is Mickey's face this early on a Saturday morning. "I know you're pissed but just take a second and think about what it is that you ultimately want before you say the wrong thing."

"I know exactly what I want to say to that old crow. Let me at her!" Mickey shouts. They definitely know she's here now.

"Mickey, let me handle this for you. Please, go back downstairs and I will talk to Mrs. Esop, okay?" Not that I'm really feeling this approach but the last thing I want is the cops called.

"Fine, Jayd. I want a copy of the agreement she made me sign. I think we need to change a few things." Mickey's smile says victory but I know she's not that gullible to think that Nigel having one fight with a woman beater is going to turn the tables completely in her favor. It's not

Nigel's fault that David can't take punches like the ones he throws at Nellie.

"Okay. I got it."

I watch Mickey descend back down the staircase like she owns this house and everything in it. That's how she walked around when she was big and pregnant with another dude's baby. Mrs. Esop got her back then and I'm sure she's already working on a master plan to get her back now.

I knock on the large French doors and wait for Mrs. Esop to answer, which she finally does.

"Jayd. What brings you by this morning?" she says, pulling her drapes open. Her garden is always a sight to behold. "Did Natasia reel you in to be a part of her bridal party?"

"No ma'am, not exactly." I step further into the waiting area of the massive bedroom and notice that her husband's side of the bed looks untouched. It also looks like Mrs. Esop's been crying all night long. Maybe Mickey does have her right where she wants her with this new development. "Mickey wants to have an attorney look over the agreement and asks that you give it to me for her."

"Yes, I heard," Mrs. Esop says, gazing out of the window. "All I ever wanted was for Natasia to be happy. She will always be my baby girl, no matter how unrecognizable she is to me."

Mrs. Esop sounds so much like Chase's mom a few months ago that I almost feel sorry for her, but not that sorry. Unlike Mrs. Carmichael, most of her drama is completely self-created.

"Mrs. Esop, I'm sorry that y'all are going through so much but all I'm here for are those papers. I have to get to work so if you want me to I can come back for them later."

"No need to come back for them, Jayd," she says, opening the antique desk drawer next to the bay window and taking out the documents. "Do you know the downside to having money, power and prestige?" Mrs. Esop says while signing on the multiple dotted lines. Think of how many trees died over this made up bull she's put into motion. I'm just glad Mickey's finally agreed to let Mrs. Carmichael read over the agreement and do damage control like the professional attorney that she is.

"No, I don't since I've never had any of those attributes."

"Well, consider yourself lucky in more ways than one. The downside is that you never know when people want to associate with you or your wealth. And that's what I like about you, Jayd. You seem to

176

care less about my money and access to a world I know you belong in. Such a pity, really. I think we make quite an admirable team." Mrs. Esop places the documents in a manila folder and hands it to me. "You and your little friend are now free of me and my influence, just like my children."

Damn, now I feel like shit. I know Mrs. Esop means well, she just goes about it all wrong.

"Thank you." I turn around ready to make my exit but I can't leave her like this. "And I want you to know that I do appreciate what you tried to do for me. Honestly, I just don't understand why you did it the way that you did."

She looks at me almost mournfully before retreating back into her king-sized bed. I guess it's like Mama said: Material things are easy to come by. What matters most is the relationships we make along the way and from what I can see, Mrs. Esop's a very lonely woman.

When I get back downstairs Rah's in the foyer calming Nigel down. This is the first time that I've laid eyes on him since our dream escapades began weeks ago. I'm glad that Chase left before Rah arrived. If there's one more confrontation this morning I think I'm going to snap.

"Where's Mickey?" I ask, looking around. I know she didn't just up and leave me here to clean up her mess.

"In hell I pray." Damn, Nigel's on one today, for real. "I'll be back." Nigel takes the stairs two at a time and reaches the top in seconds.

"You can't speak?" Rah says, now that we're alone.

"Rah, I really don't have time for this." Instead of allowing my protest, Rah steps up to me and kisses me on my neck. Well that's one way to say hello.

"Rah, I can't." I back away from him and put my hands out in front of me.

Rah looks genuinely hurt by my actions. "Jayd, tell me that you have dreams with someone else like the ones we share." I guess he does remember them.

"That's not the point, Rah," I whisper. I don't need everyone up in our business. "No matter how much you try and rationalize it, me being your side piece will never make sense to me."

"Jayd, it's not my fault. You know I love you, girl," Rah says, pulling me into his embrace. "Everything else is just a formality. I love you too much to ever let you go. You bring out a part of me that I never knew I had. That shit's not common, girl. And besides that, you are the finest Queen I've ever seen."

Rah pulls me closer, kisses my nose, my top lip, and then my whole mouth. I surrender to his energy. I know I love this brotha. He is my first love, my first hate, my best friend, and my brother. He is also someone I've been attracted to for as long as I can remember, and his kisses are everything to me.

"I can't lie. The dreams we've been sharing are more of a reality than the real deal," I say, in between kisses. "But they also scare me because I don't want to wake up from them."

"I know exactly how you feel," Rah says, holding me tighter than before. "I always feel like we wake up too soon."

I let him distract me again and love every minute of it. But I can't stay this way. Mama's stories about she and Dr. Whitmore's tainted love flash to the front of my thoughts. I can't keep Rah, not like this.

"Let's take this back to my place," Rah says, moving his lips back down to my neck.

I consider his offer and then snap back into the moment. "No. I wish that everything could be like it is in our dreams but it's not."

"What's stopping us right now from making it a reality?"

"What's stopping me is that never in our dreams was I the other woman," I say, releasing myself from his embrace.

"You're not the other woman, Jayd. You're the first woman. Always have been and always will be."

My God, he's making so much sense this morning. He must have just finished reading an Iceberg Slim book for the umpteenth time.

"I have to get to work, Rah." I look at the wall clock and notice that I'm going to be late if I don't catch the bus within the next ten minutes. Mama and Netta have been more than patient with my decision to stick it out at Simply Wholesome, but I can't be late on the days I do agree to show up.

"Jayd, come on girl. You've got a minute for me, maybe two if we do it right."

"No Rah, don't. Besides, Nigel needs you and I need to find Mickey." If she hasn't taken off already she can give me a ride to Compton whether she's going that way or not. After all of the mess she's involved me in she owes me a ride or two.

"Did you get the papers or what?" Mickey says, stepping out of the kitchen bathroom and scaring the shit out of me and Rah.

"Damn, Mickey. What are you doing in here?" Rah asks. "I don't think Nigel wants to see you right now."

"Good, because I don't want to see his ass, either. You can tell that little punk that I'll see him soon. Know what I'm saying?"

Rah looks utterly confused by her smug attitude, which means there's more to the story than I know. I don't think Mickey realizes she's poking an angry bull in the nose but something tells me that she's about to find out.

"Let's go, Mickey. We can talk about this on the way to Compton."

I push Mickey toward the front door and say my good byes to Rah. I'm sure I'll see him in my dreams at some point, but it was still good to lay eyes on him.

Because Mickey opted to take Slauson to the 110 freeway, I convinced her to stop at Mama's favorite fish spot, which also happens to be near one of Rah's mom's many former houses. No matter where I go I don't think I can ever fully escape Rah's pull. Carson's a bit out of the way but not too far and it was definitely worth it. It's about time I treated my godmother and grandmother to a meal for a change. And as busy as our Saturday was we all deserve a break from the kitchen.

"Don't get me wrong, when your grandfather and I first met I couldn't keep my hands off of him," Mama says in between bites. I got her favorites: catfish nuggets and red snapper. Netta and I both love shrimp and hush puppies, so I got a big basket for each of us. Netta had to run an errand and left me and Mama to eat by ourselves.

"Mama, please," I say, nearly losing my appetite.

"Please what? If more grown women talked to growing young women about men and things they'd be better off in so many ways."

I think about Mickey and her mom's lack of talking and can't help but agree. Mama is always right when she's right.

"Your grandfather was a great lover and yes we had fun outside of the bedroom, too. But it was Dr. Whitmore who knew how to love my mind body and soul: the Holy Trinity for real."

"For real?" I say feeling the heat rise in my body. The fact that Rah can dream with me is more intimate than anyone else can ever get with me because I feel him on so many levels. So why the hell can't we just be together?

"Because life is not a straight road," Mama says, snatching up my thought. "There are many twists and turns and you just have to move with them or snap. Look at Sandy. She's broke, much like Pam was, bless her heart. But Sandy didn't have to be. She could have fled from her past. Instead she chose to obsess over something she couldn't have anymore. Whatever you do, Jayd, don't get stuck in the past."

Cameron and Jeremy are stuck. Mickey and her man are definitely stuck. Sandy and Trish and Rah are trapped in a strange and sordid superglue, and Nigel is stuck on Mickey, much like Nellie is on Chase and Nigel. Me, I guess I'm stuck on stupid because I made life much more complicated than it needs to be.

"What do you think of me and Chase making it official?" I ask just to throw it out there.

Mama thinks carefully before answering. "I like Chase, and I like Chase for you. But he is not the one for you in that way, but he was a good first lover for you to have. If Rah was your first I don't know how sane you would have been after that encounter."

She's on point with that assessment. If our dreams are driving me crazy, I can only imagine what would happen if we actually did make them a reality. I'd probably be off the chain like his baby-mama Sandy's crazy ass. She and Trish are whipped over Rah, so much so that I'm cool with staying in the dark about how he gets down in real life. I don't have time for another breakdown.

"I read this book years ago, 'Like Water for Chocolate' and I saw the movie many times after that. It talks about how a fire denied will combust rapidly and passionately, which I think you and Rah are not ready for. He's in fear of being deemed a bad parent and a bad man.

He's carrying the weight of the world on his shoulders and no one's asked him to," Mama says, dipping her fish into the small container of tartar sauce. "He was born with his ancestor's burdens and chooses to live out that path. That path has no space for a fire child like you, Jayd. Not right now. Your ancestors are calling on you as well. And, like Rah, you have to heed their calls."

I knew there was a reason that Rah and I have always been in sync.

"What about Jeremy?" I know that's a loaded question but I might as well get him out of the way, too. I already know how they feel about Keenan so no need to go there.

"What about him?" Mama answers, matter-of-factly. "That child made his own bed. Now he has to lie in it, without you."

Damn, that leaves me with no one, or at least no one that I've met yet. "How come I feel like the ones that I choose never fully choose me back?"

"Because you have to choose yourself first," Mama says. "Until then, you'll always look for someone else's approval and love. There's nothing easier to take advantage of than someone else's insecurity. Look at Nellie. That girl has made bad choices time and time again, and Mickey and Rah and Chase and the list goes on, baby. As long as we continue to seek love outside of the true source of all love it will always hurt."

"That makes perfect sense," I say, swallowing my tears, and the rest of my hush puppies.

"You know what else makes sense, Jayd?" Mama says, taking one of my shrimp.

"What's that?"

"Telling your grandmother when you're going to do something as brazen as to go after her oldest and most formidable enemy all by your little lonesome."

Damn, I guess the cat's out of the bag with or without my bracelets. "Mama, it's not like that."

"Oh really? Well, please do share what it's actually like because from what I saw going on in that little teenaged brain of yours it was that and then some. And how exactly do you think that you and your little friends were going to get away with this plan of yours? Have you not learned a thing from living next door to that woman for all of these years?"

"Mama, we've got it under control." The last thing I want is Mama to intervene on my behalf. She's not completely healed from her last encounter with Esmeralda. Even with the protection we cast on her, I don't know if she can take another hit.

"Jayd, I know that you think you do but trust me, baby. Esmeralda can see you coming a mile away. Ask your mother if you don't believe me, or have you forgotten what it's like when Esmeralda gets inside of your head?"

"I'm not my mom," I say, coolly. I resent the comparison, but no need to throw gasoline on the fire.

"Oh no? Could've fooled me with this move, Jayd. You've lost your ever-loving mind if you think that you and a couple of local drug dealers can take her and her house down, not to mention Hector's role in all of this."

"Mama," I start, even though I know my words are practically meaningless at this point. "I wanted to protect you. She's out for blood, your blood, and she won't stop until she gets it."

"Jayd, I appreciate you wanting to protect me, I really do. But this isn't the way to get it done, baby. You should never put yourself in harms way for me."

"Understood." I agree to end the conversation but there's no way that I'm going to stop what's already in motion.

I thought that I could leave my bracelets on when I'm around my family but it looks like I need to stay on my solo mission day and night. The last thing I need is them up in my head when I'm kicking Esmeralda's ass, which should be right around the corner. According to Pete, Hector's been acting very evasive since our special delivery this morning and that's exactly the way we want it. The less help Esmeralda has the better. Even if Mama disagrees, her takedown is imminent. I just have to keep everyone off my trail until after I get the job done.

"I know it's difficult sticking out in a crowd, especially at school, but it's worth it."
- Lynn Marie
Drama High, volume 6: Courtin' Jayd

~ 13 ~
DREAMCATCHER

Instead of folks taking their kids to church with them today it seemed like everyone just wanted to get their kids' hair braided for the upcoming week. I had to cut my nails to speed up my braiding process but I don't really mind. I also type better with no nails and that will help with the mountain of homework I have to catch up on including my research for the off campus debate tomorrow, which completely slipped my mind. If it were any other teacher except Mr. Adewale I'd pull out of the competition, but I'm not going to be the one to disappoint him.

"Hello, Jayd," my mom says, dumping her overflowing laundry basket in the middle of the living room floor. "I can see someone's been busy today."

"Yeah, too busy to do my own hair and I still have a ton of schoolwork to do," I say, catching my tore up reflection in the mirror.

"Maybe you should just wear it slicked back until you have more time for yourself. I hate to be the one to tell you this but you're looking a little busted, honey."

"Thanks, mom." My feelings would be hurt but I know she's

telling the truth. I've been feeling very plain lately, like I'm letting myself go in a way. I've just been too distracted to care.

"Oh baby, I only say it because I love you, and because it's the truth." She bends down over the basket to sort her laundry.

"I know, mom. I want to change my look up, maybe get a haircut or something. I don't know."

"Now you know a child of Oshune can't cut her hair except under the most serious of circumstances. How about some highlights instead?" My mom steps behind me in the mirror and touches the ends of my hair. "What's up with the little kid earrings?"

"I usually put studs in both holes when I have to do kids' hair," I say, touching the rhinestones. "I learned my lesson the hard way the last time I braided Rahima's hair." I do miss Rah's little girl.

"How's working at Simply Wholesome going?" my mom asks as she eyes the balls of hair on the living room carpet.

"It's going," I say, sweeping the kitchen floor before moving onto the rest of the small apartment. "Training is taking forever because of all of the stuff with Mama, not to mention the fact that I can only train one day out of the week because of Summer's schedule. She's really busy and so am I."

"I understand that but seriously, Jayd. You need to make training there a priority. The sooner you can move your business out of my house the better."

"Mom, you're not even here most of the time," I say, reiterating Mama's point. "Why do you care so much?"

"I care because when I am here the last thing I need is to run into little kids and their mamas. And I'd also like to come home to a clean apartment, if that's okay with you."

"I hear you, mom, and I'm working on it as fast as I can." Why is she on my ass to get a move on all of a sudden?

"By the way, have you figured out what you're going to do this summer when my lease is up?"

"Hopefully I'll be living on campus by then." Which campus I don't know, but wherever it is will have to be heavily subsidized because funds are tighter than ever.

I still have to figure out a way to get my mom's car fixed. Yesterday she informed me that she doesn't want to report it to the insurance agency again for fear of our premiums increasing and I feel her on that one. So now I'm back to square one in that regard.

I hate to admit it, but seeing Rah yesterday made me realize that I really do miss his friendship on so many levels. If he could truly be just a friend that would be optimal, but from the shit he pulled yesterday there's little chance of that happening.

"You need to talk to your dad about that. He should help you pay for college if you get in somewhere, and your housing too."

"What do you mean 'if I get in'?" I ask, a bit insulted.

"I'm just saying that it's very competitive these days, that's all. Just make sure that you have a back-up plan, baby, like doing hair at Simply Wholesome. I'm off to the laundry mat. Bye, love."

"Bye, mom." I'm sure that she doesn't mean to pimp slap a sister's dreams, but she does it all of the time without even knowing.

College was never that important to my mother and I know that she thinks high school is really the end of "needed" education. Getting a job, finding a man, and kicking it with her girlfriends may be satisfactory for the rest of her life but not mine. First of all, my friends are not reliable and neither are the so-called men that I choose. For me, school is my only stable companion and we still have a long way to go.

Last night I chose to stay at my mom's apartment and catch up on some much needed me time. In between studying I deep conditioned my hair with some of my homemade honey soufflé conditioner and I'm glad that I did. Nothing feels better than a clean head. I even had a nice dream that didn't involve screaming out Rah's name. I dreamt that I was in college, living in the dorms and actually experiencing a normal life for once. I don't know if the dreamcatcher that Mama made for me to keep in my travel bag when I was younger was working overtime last night or what, but it was nice to wake up refreshed and guilt-free. I should start my weeks off like this every Monday.

South Bay High's debate team has been holding its own during our first competition but it hasn't been easy. Our competitors have been doing this in their sleep for years and we all look like we just woke up, including Reid who was ousted in the first round. We are on the second to last round now and I'm still hanging in but I don't know how much longer I can keep it up.

There's one cat that's just outright impressive in both intellect and stature. Dude is on point with his verbal skills and he's not bad looking, either. I can't tell if he's black or not, but he's got the swag of a brotha and I definitely like what I see and hear.

"Mr. Muhammad, the floor is yours." Muhammad. I wonder if he's Muslim, and if so can he date a sistah outside of his religion? For a brotha that fine I might even consider converting. There's nothing wrong with dual religious citizenship.

"South Bay's Jayd Jackson and Westingle's Ishaq Muhammad will spar in the final round. You have ten minutes to prepare."

He would be from Westingle, Rah and Nigel's high school before he transferred to South Bay. There's just something about the brothas on the west side.

"Miss Jackson, you'll have the rebuttal. Make South Bay proud," Mr. Adewale says, officially causing my nerves to rattle. He's been glowing all day, apparently very proud of the way that I'm carrying myself. Several other students decided not to show up and with Reid sulking somewhere, I realize that I'm our last hope.

I walk outside of the stuffy classroom and look across Sunset Boulevard at the picturesque campus across the street. It feels like I've already been a student there before. I'd remember that no matter which life it was in. Keenan's so fortunate to be a student athlete at one of the top universities in the country, and so are Nigel and KJ for being given the opportunity to attend. Normal students like me getting into a school like UCLA is a crapshoot at best.

"Isn't it beautiful?" Mr. Adewale says, standing next to me. "I've always wanted to go to grad school there."

"Yes, very." I've never dreamed of going to a school like UCLA, mostly because I never knew anyone who got in before this year.

"You should start filling out your applications soon if you didn't head my last warning, Jayd. It's also part of your AP requirements this year, essays and all, just in case Mrs. Bennett didn't inform you."

"Seriously?" I ask. I'm just getting used to the idea of being a senior. College used to seem so far away but it's literally right in front of me.

"Yes, Jayd. Seriously," he says, concerned. "You've been a bit distant lately. Everything okay?"

"Nothing I can't handle."

"Well, just know that I'm here if you need me. And don't worry about your grandmother, Jayd. You know Dr. Whitmore is on the case."

I bet he is. "I know Mama's protected," I say, relaxing a bit. I sometimes forget that my favorite teacher is also my spiritual god brother. And he's been a bit distant lately himself. There's always more work to do than time so I get it. Honestly, I like him better on a personal level. He's one of the most difficult teachers that I've ever had and he's been riding me to finish my applications. One thing at a time is all I can handle.

"It's time," one of the moderators announces, calling us back into the competition.

"Okay, Jayd. You've got this. Just remember to site your evidence and slow down. I know that you think you're not talking fast but sometimes you're moving a mile a minute."

"I hear you." Just like in real life, I suppose. Being patient isn't my strong suit and working with Sin Piedad is using up all of my reserves. The hardest thing is waiting for the results when I've already done part of the work. We can't move forward until we know that Esmeralda's been affected and taken the bait that Hector should've delivered by now. As Netta would say, all I've got control over is this moment, and right now there's a cute guy who needs to be verbally humbled by my fiery words.

"You don't know what the Creator has in store for you."
-Lynn Marie
Drama High, volume 14: So, So Hood

~14~
SIREN

After seeing Keenan's school the other day I decided to give him a call. I'm patiently waiting for Keenan to get off of work so that we can hang out for a bit, so why do I feel like I'm part of the crew? I need to come up on their tips if that's the case. The glass jar is full of money both that jingles and folds. Luckily they're not in my neck of the woods. Otherwise that jar would mysteriously disappear on a daily basis.

The burger spot on the corner of Market and La Brea in Inglewood used to keep a tip jar beside the cash register. It started walking away and then they moved it to the counter, where it also developed legs. Soon there was no tip jar at all, only very irritated workers behind the register. I'd be irritated too if what little tips I worked so hard for were stolen by the very people who are supposed to be leaving them in the first place.

"Hey baby," Keenan says. I look around to make sure he's talking to me. Baby? Are we there already and I didn't know it?

"Nice to see you too, sweet dumpling," I say, making Keenan's already big smile grow even wider. "How's your day going?" I place my backpack down on the table closest to the coffee bar. Keenan likes to chat while he works and I enjoy the light conversation. I'm glad his schedule allows him to work on my early day this week. Usually I'd be at the shop with Netta and Mama but sometimes on slow days they like to be alone. I don't mind the day off.

"Excellent, except my study group showed up unexpectedly. They're demanding an impromptu session while I'm working, which is not what's up. They're lucky I'm a forgiving person," Keenan says, tossing a balled up napkin at the table behind us.

"Hey, watch it Mr. Washington," a very pale white boy in glasses and all black attire says, tossing the paper back to Keenan who catches it like a football. Keenan Washington is a nice name. I wonder what's his middle name? "This is harassment and a law suit waiting to happen."

I've yet to see him play in a game even though he keeps inviting me. Too bad my weekends are always full of work. Otherwise I'd be a proud fan on the sidelines.

"Jayd, this is Walter. Walter, this is my friend, Jayd."

"Charmed, I'm sure," Walter says, reaching for my hand to shake. "Please excuse me for a moment. It seems that nature's calling and I must obey."

And I thought that my friends were full of drama. I can already tell

197

that he's a lot to deal with.

"I was near your school on Monday," I say, returning my attention to Keenan who's on to the next customer's drink order.

"Really? And you didn't let me know? We could've had lunch or something."

"I wish but it was an afterschool sponsored visit. We had a debate competition at the high school across the street."

"Ah, yes. Speech and debate," Keenan says, nostalgically. "I used to enjoy that elective very much."

"I bet you did."

"So, how did we do?"

"We won second place for student congress, and I took home first place for spar and debate." I have to admit I'm also still spinning from the unexpected victory. It felt good claiming my trophy, especially since no one else thought I would win, least of all Reid. Haven't they learned by now not to doubt me?

"Damn, Jayd. Way to go," Keenan says, proud of my accomplishment.

"Once I graduate from law school I'm going to sue this establishment for the lack of proper accessories in the men's restroom," Walter says with wet hands.

"Walter, you know you're not going to law school. It's too much like real work no matter how much your grandfather wants you take over the family firm," Keenan says, making the entire table laugh—all except for Walter.

"I resent that statement, young lad." Walter says.

Keenan looks at him with a knowing smirk.

"The gentleman doth protest too much, me thinks," an equally pale white girl says, adding her own spin to the Shakespearean quote. Luckily my tenth grade English teacher Mrs. Malone made sure we read all of the classics, including Hamlet. "You are a born actor, my love," she says, touching Walter's forearm like she owns it.

"Jocelyn, I think you and Walter both protest too much about all the wrong things," a young, Latin brother says. "We need to get this scene done or I'll never be able to sleep tonight. A boy needs his beauty rest to be this fabulous, honey."

"Mateo, please stop," Jocelyn says, over his drama.

"Keenan, don't you agree that the psychology of Jim and Jane Doe must be thoroughly examined by Rochester in the opening scene?" Walter asks, returning Jocelyn's affection. "Otherwise my dear, sweet, young Mateo, how is the audience going to know the exact motivation for the heinous nature of his crimes?"

Mateo looks like he wants to choke Walter in good humor. "They'll know because there are two acts in the play," Mateo says, tossing his pencil on the table in jest. "A good script lets the reader participate in the character development, not show them everything up front."

"Yes, but look at Death of a Salesman," Keenan says, making a perfect cappuccino while simultaneously participating in the spirited debate. "Miller doesn't hide the woes of the main character until the second act. We know who we're getting from jump."

"You have to let certain aspects of the play reveal themselves later on. I think it's a mistake to let our audience see too much in the beginning. The mystery is what keeps them hooked until the very end." Mateo rises dramatically from his seat, whips his multi colored Louis Vuitton scarf from the right side of his neck to the left and then returns to his seat, satisfied that he's made his point.

"Fine," Jocelyn says, jotting something down in her spiral notebook. "The only way to solve this is to see the scene acted out. Walter should perform on camera with and without the psychiatrist, Mateo. Agreed?"

"Agreed," Mateo and Walter both say.

Keenan looks less than enthusiastic.

"Keenan, we'll need to shoot it this evening so we can have time to perform it one more time before we turn the assignment in on Thursday."

Keenan glances at the wall clock and then back down at me. "I'm sorry about this, Jayd. We have to shoot a thirty second piece based off the larger written work, but my group's acting like we're going out for a major picture debut. Like the shit's going to be Oscar worthy or something," he says, cracking a smile. "I'm responsible for the editing and graphics and I just want to make sure they've got the lighting down. Want to come with us? It'll only take a minute then we can go eat. Are you down for Ethiopian?"

"I'm always down for dinner but I really should be getting home, Keenan. I just wanted to drop by and say hi anyway, so no biggie," I say, trying to evade his irresistible eyes. I know I need to say no but every part of me wants to say yes.

"Come on, Jayd. I know you've missed all of this." I have to admit Keenan does make me laugh and there's no sense in going home early to an empty house. I'm still giving Chase the space he needs to forgive my midnight marauding. Maybe I'll stay at my mom's place again tonight. I'm not a fan of the early morning bus ride to Redondo Beach but it is what it is.

"Yeah, Jayd. You should come to campus with us. You can be an extra," Jocelyn says.

"Why not?" Walter says. "On second thought, no she can't. She's too busty and she's wearing too many bright colors for the camera. Why so much white and yellow, Jayd?"

"That was a bit harsh," Jocelyn says, pinching Walter's arm.

"No, it's cool. I have a full agenda myself but thanks for the invite anyway," I say, tired of the pretentious college students. Is this what it's going to be like at UCLA?

"Jayd, don't leave. Come on, just stay here and study if you don't want to come to campus with me," he says, putting his hand on my backpack. "I promise, I'll be back as soon as I can and we can grab a bite."

"Seriously, Keenan. I have so much studying to catch up on and I need to start filling out my college applications. I don't even know how I'm going to afford college but I still have to go through the steps, and there are lots of them."

"Believe me, I feel you, Jayd. That's why you should let me help you. I'm pretty good at this kind of stuff, you know." Keenan smiles that wide, bright grin of his and I return the vibe. But the majority of the work that I need to do can't be done on a laptop.

"Another time, Keenan. It was nice meeting you all," I say to his friends. With my things in hand I get up from the table and head for the front door.

"Let me walk you out." Keenan comes from behind the counter and follows me to the front of the café. The evening is setting in. In a little while it'll be dark and I want to be home before that happens.

"Thanks for the coffee, Keenan. It was good seeing you."

"It was good seeing you too, Miss Jackson. And I'm serious about your applications. I can help you register for your exams and fill out your FAFSA too," Keenan says, inciting even more panic in me. The applications are enough work. I hadn't given much thought to everything else.

"I'd appreciate that. Just let me know when you're free and I'll work it out." Thank God he knows what he's talking about.

"For sure. And you know, Jayd, there's more scholarship money from Alpha Gamma Ro where that came from. They have another award, which pays a student's tuition for up to four years at any four-year accredited college or university, granted she becomes a little sister until she's able to pledge," he says, parroting Mrs. Esop. "Obviously the institution must have access to one of the chapters, but that's not difficult since they are one of the largest sororities in the world."

203

"Is there anything you don't know about when it comes to all things college?" I am impressed with his willingness to help me through the process. As behind as I am I'm going to need all the help I can get.

"I don't know all things, just the most important things," Keenan says, touching the tip of my nose with the back of his forefinger. "There's a party this weekend at the African Student Union on campus. As president of your school's club, it might good for you to network with some college students. Bring your friends if they're interested. Well, not all of your friends. Just the serious ones." Mickey has certainly left a bad taste in his mouth from the last party.

"We have some other things planned this weekend, but I'll let you know." Like I don't already know that I'll be taking over Esmeralda's world, but maybe I can drop by after.

Although Keenan did come to Pam's going home celebration, he doesn't know much about my spirit life and I'm in no rush to tell him all about my crazy life. I like having a friend outside of my high school identity and family drama.

"You do that, Jayd. Get home safely." He kisses me on the cheek and opens the door. As we walk out we notice several regular customers for this time of day, including a mom who always seems out of it along with her unruly toddler. Why is she leaving a stack of unsupervised twenty-dollar bills on the corner of the coffee table with her opened purse while her wild two-year old spreads eagle across the floor and throws her keys under the chair? I wish Rahima would pull some shit like that. Her daddy would have her ass before he'd let her get away with that type of behavior in public or at home.

Keenan watches the spectacle and smiles knowing that I feel him. All I have to do is deal with the people; Keenan has to work around this privileged crew all week long. If it weren't for the tips and the need to pay bills I'm sure he would've bounced a long time ago.

"Keenan, I thought you'd be here," a tall, black chick says, interrupting our goodbyes. She walks over to Keenan and kisses him on the lips.

What the hell?

Keenan turns beet red and stops short of giving her the same greeting he gave me when I first arrived. My mom, grandmother, and Netta were right about him. I now know that I've been played like the silly high school girl he's taken me for.

"I have to go," I say, walking out on him and his college chick.

"Oh, I didn't mean to intrude," she says, genuinely flustered. "I can't stay but I just wanted to make sure I checked on you, Keenan. Is everything okay?" She looks at me and then at Keenan who doesn't

205

know what to say.

"Like I said, I have to go."

"I'll just be a second," Keenan says to his apparent boo.

She walks over to the table and takes a seat with the rest of his friends. The other students who a moment ago were cool toward me are dead silent out of loyalty to their boy and his apparently trifling ways, just like a real crew should be.

Before I can fully escape, Nellie's boyfriend walks into the coffee house with very visible bruises to his face and body.

"Hey, Keenan," David says, walking straight to the bar. I don't think he even noticed me. His family's church isn't too far from here and this is one of the best hangouts on this side of town.

"How do you know David?" I ask Keenan before I make a mad dash to the bus stop up the block.

"He's in the freshman exchange program, and my parents attend his father's church from time to time. He's cool. A little volatile at bible study sometimes, but still cool."

"He's beating Nellie." I didn't mean to blurt that out but how else should I say something like that?

Keenan looks unmoved by my statement. "I doubt that, seriously. Besides, your girl could use being humbled a bit."

"What the hell is that supposed to mean?"

"It means that she's got a mouth on her, just like your other friend Mickey. No man wants to hear that shit all day and she's high maintenance. Nellie's just an all around bad combo. Ugh!"

Without hesitation the palm of my right hand meets with Keenan's left cheek. Time seems to have stopped as Keenan and I stand still in the shock of the moment. I would apologize for the thoughtless action but regardless of my state of mind, I don't feel sorry.

"Seriously, Jayd? Did you just try to slap me, girl?"

"I think it was more than a try."

"What the hell did you do that for?" he asks, rubbing his face. If his skin feels anything like mine the heat is just setting in.

Honestly, I don't know why I hit him. I'm usually not a violent person but my tolerance is at an all-time low. I have no patience to debate with him about why his comments about Nellie are so stupid. My action showed him what my words couldn't. I slapped him for David and G; for my trifling uncles who keep giving my grandmother a hard time; for Misty and Emilio who just won't sit down somewhere; and most of all for Rah who has way too many infractions to name.

"Sorry. I just had a flashback of Ray and Janay Rice fighting in that hotel elevator. You should watch the video again. I think your boy over there tried to do his own live reenactment on my girl."

And with that I'm out. As hot as I am right now there's no going back to Inglewood for the night. I need to get to the spirit room and work on my own shit, including putting David in his place. If Nellie wants to make an enemy out of me, so be it. But I'm not letting my former girl go out like that, frenemies be damned.

"Crazy is where your power lies."
-Netta
Drama High, volume 13: The Meltdown

~ 15 ~
H.A.M.

"Here baby. Have some dinner," I say, placing the hot cast-iron pot in the middle of the dining room table. I remove the lid with a potholder and pour out some stew for my husband.

"Thank you, my love." He places the cloth napkin I spent hours sewing across his lap and claims his soupspoon. "It's delicious," he says, loudly slurping.

"I'm glad you like it." I roll up the sleeves on the colonial dress to reveal my bleeding wrist. "I made it extra special for you this evening, mon amour."

"I can tell," my husband says without looking up. It isn't until he notices the white carpet studded with maroon drops that he stops eating to look at me. "My love, what have you done?" He looks into the bowl of red stew and allows it to slip from his fingers. The stew joins the red stains below.

"I've given you what you've always wanted, no? To watch me die slowly while you sleep with woman after woman in New Orleans! Go ahead. Eat up," I say, taking the pot and throwing it up against the wall

where its contents drip down the walls and stain the curtains and everything else in its path. "This is the last time that I'll bleed over you, do you hear me?"

My husband catches me as I fall to the ground but I'm not the only one feeling ill.

"What's wrong with me?" he asks, grabbing at his chest. "I, I can't breathe. My love, what have you done?"

"We'll be together in death as we should've been in life, mon amour."

We both succumb to our shared fates: him, baffled and me, satisfied. "Til death do us part."

On the nearly two-hour bus ride to Compton I had plenty of time to think about my string of bad luck with dudes thanks to the disturbing dream that interrupted a good nap. I've come to the conclusion that it's not them, it's me. I need a break from it all. They keep my head up in the clouds when I need my feet planted firmly on the ground. I simply don't have the time to stay caught up in romantic notions of loyalty and forgiveness and all of the other bull that fairytales dish out.

Walking up the long, winding block I can recall playing hopscotch on these very same sidewalks when I was a child. Even then I had problems with the kids in the neighborhood. And, even then I hated Esmeralda. Houses glow with their evening light and a few of the neighbors sit on their porches smoking cigarettes and catching up on the daily gossip. The closer I get to the middle of the block the more clearly I can hear Mama's yelling.

I break into a sprint and reach the open back door where I have to duck in order to avoid getting hit.

"That's it! I've had it!" Mama yells at the top of her lungs. "I'm done being disrespected in this woman-forsaken house! Take it all. Y'all can have it!" Mama takes the hot pot off of the stove and throws it bottom-up in the sink. Spaghetti sauce splashes, speckling the curtains and the dingy yellow wall behind it, just like in my dream. But instead of it being blood it's just food and I'm so glad it is.

"Mama, be careful. You're going to burn yourself," I say, handing her a towel but she's unreachable when her head gets this hot. As cool as she was with Netta's pin firmly in place is exactly how hot she is now.

"Jayd, let's go and get my overnight bag out of the closet and pack it good. I'm leaving this house once and for all." Mama takes her apron off and throws it in the sink, too.

"Mama, what happened?" I ask, following her to the bedroom.

"The trifling ass men in this house have no respect. And I'll be damned if I spend another minute cleaning up after their grown asses, you hear me? Not another goddamn minute!"

"Okay, Mama. I'll get your things ready." I assume she's going back to Dr. Whitmore's office but how are we going to get there? I know Daddy's not going to take us when he gets home and I don't want to bother Netta this time of night. Mama's not sick, just pissed.

"We're going to the back house for now, Jayd," Mama says, putting my mind at ease. "I'll work the rest out tomorrow, and so will you."

I guess she can feel the heat on my head too. The Williams' women can't seem to catch a break lately and I doubt it's a coincidence. I don't think my plan with Esmeralda can wait until this weekend. I have to finish this, even if I have to go buck wild on her ass all by myself.

While meditating this morning I prayed for the ability to pray like our mothers, the elder women in all white at the front of the church, the women in the community who would take over your house when trouble or illness came to the household, women like my godmother and grandmother. I want to learn how to be prayer warriors like them.

There was a bible verse inside of my spirit notebook that stuck out and I memorized it. "When I was a child, I talked like a child, I thought like a child, I reasoned like a child. When I became a man, I put the ways of childhood behind me." I took that and many other spiritual verses to heart when I decided to come back to Compton and get to work on tonight's festivities. I met with Mauricio, Javier and Pete to let them know that I decided to move on Esmeralda tonight and they weren't feeling it at all, especially since they haven't heard from Chase in two days. He's not returning any of my calls, either. I was worried and called his mom who said that he's been home every night, so I guess he's just going through it. Technically, he did his part for the time being. It's up to me to finish the plan.

I need to stay focused in order to stay on task but unfortunately Mickey decided to show up with her own set of issues ending my peaceful preparation. She and G got wind of my meeting with Sin Piedad today and decided to drill me about it. Instead of telling her about their plans to end G's slanging of the wrong shit, I tell them about Esmeralda's mind control game on him. The more soldiers I have up in arms on my side, the better.

"Oh hell nah, Jayd. If what you're saying is true, then us not going after them sadistic bitches is not happening," Mickey says, passing a screaming Nickey to me, ready to ride out like a true ride or die chick. Not that I don't love spending time with my godbaby, but Mickey's lost

213

her mind if she thinks I have time to babysit while she gets her ass kicked.

"I know you're ready to ride for G but are you ready to die? Because that's exactly what's going to happen one way or another if you walk into that house," I say, passing her daughter back to her. If she had any sense at all she would've left Nickey at home with her mother.

"You should know by now that I'll do anything for my boo," Mickey says. I know her loyalty is more out of guilt than righteousness. She's been a client of Esmeralda's in the past and I doubt she's shared that fact with G.

"My grandma told me to stay away from that house," G says, taking out his cell. It's hard for me to imagine G as a little boy named Gary with a grandma. "I always did but not tonight. Me and my boys are going to light that house up, and that's not up for negotiation."

"But G, I'm telling you I saw it," I plead. The last thing I want is more blood on my hands. We need to humble Esmeralda, not kill her or anyone else if it can be avoided. "I had a vision about a doll that looked like you under her control. For all you know she could be manipulating you right now."

"Come on, baby. I told you she wouldn't be on our side, as always," Mickey says, giving me the evil eye. Mickey and Nickey get back into the car while G walks across the driveway to visit my neighbor.

Mauricio and Javier pull up in front of Esmeralda's house with a crew of their own. Oh hell no they're not bringing this shit to my street. I thought they were going to handle this the same way that I am—in the spirit world or at least at Hector's crib. Esmeralda should be just about ready to leave for the bembe at his house and that's when I'm going to make my move.

"What up, fool?" G says, approaching the tricked out SUV.

"What's up is that a little birdie told me and my partners that you were partnering up with an old lady to take over our territory and sell nonorganics to our people," Mauricio says. "Say it ain't so, G."

"You know what, fool?" G says, not backing down. "She's the one who's got this shit on lock, not my niggas and me."

"I don't give a shit who thought they had it on lock," Javier says, touching his side. "Long Beach owns this territory now, end of discussion. We don't sell bullshit product in our hood, you feel me?"

"Go ahead, Jayd. We got this." Mauricio says, staring G down.

I know it's time for me to go. I sprint toward the backhouse to check for Mama but she's not there. I look toward the main house and see her bedroom light's on. Maybe she needed something from inside. I just want to make sure that she's settled in before I remove my bracelets and go for Esmeralda's head.

"You look different," Mama says when I step inside her bedroom. The room is dark except for the candles burning on her corner shrine.

"Just tired, that's all. Is there anything I can get for you?" I ask, glancing at my cell for the time. "My friends are here to give me a ride back to Palos Verdes." That's not exactly true but I need to cover my basis just in case she asks what Mickey's doing here.

"No, thank you baby. Good night." Mama sits down at the foot of her bed and turns on the television—one thing that's not in the spirit room.

"Okay, Mama. I'll see you tomorrow." I kiss my grandmother on the cheek and head for the door.

"My, that's an awfully big crocodile."

"What crocodile, Mama?" I ask from the hallway. She must be watching The Discovery Channel, her favorite when she can escape work. I guess being on a fake vacation has been good for her in multiple ways.

"The one I'm riding. He says we should visit the bottom of the river," she answers, sounding more like herself in one of our shared dreams.

216

Something's wrong. I rush back into the small room and see Misty exiting the closet holding Mama's voodoo doll. Mama's sleepwalking again and Misty's at the controls. I don't have time to play with this girl.

At the risk of her hurting Mama I opt to jump into the vision with her. *"Mama, I need for you to wake up. Now, Mama. Open your eyes and come with me,"* I say, attempting to lead Mama out of the dream but she's not budging. She's too far-gone to listen to reason.

A crocodile is much bigger and stronger than an alligator, that much I know. But there's something else about the river reptile that's making me uncomfortable, a strange level of familiarity. It's Rousseau. How did he get past our protection?

"Damn, Jayd. Looks like your grandmother just flew over the cuckoo's nest," Misty says, smiling sinisterly at Mama. "She should really see someone about that."

"It's over, Misty," I say, carefully walking toward her without letting go of Mama's mind. Misty's now seated in the window seal like she hasn't got a care in the world. "Esmeralda's about to be done and so are you. Now give me the doll."

"I don't think so, Jayd. I rather like playing God," Misty says, twirling the black and gray hairs covering Mama's doll made by Esmeralda. "It's quite a rush, Jayd. You should try it sometime."

217

"I don't want to try anything Esmeralda's got a hand in." It looks like Misty's high on Ecstasy or some other drug Esmeralda's got G slanging. Her eyes are glassy and she's in an unusually good mood.

"Tsk, tsk, Jayd. You shouldn't knock anything unless you try it first. Oh, but wait a minute. Look who I'm talking to: The worlds oldest virgin." Misty lets out a roar of laughter as she continues to torment my grandmother. If she only knew how untrue that statement is, but my love life is none of her business and neither are my grandmother's dreams.

"Give me the doll, Misty!" I scream, lunging forward.

"Hell no, you stupid little bitch!" Misty says, bolting across the room and standing next to Mama who's still sleepwalking.

I reach Misty in two steps and slap the shit out of her right cheek forcing the smile off of her face. We fall to the ground as she struggles to keep the doll in her possession. She may have lost a good twenty pounds since her forced transformation but the broad's build is still as solid as mine and not easily beaten, unlike Cameron.

"Let go of my grandmother!"

"Never!" Misty attempts to escape but I've got her in a headlock and she can't go anywhere until I let her go.

"Fine. Have it your way." The heat in my head rises and begins to throb. I feel like Kanye West's *Monster* as my sight switches from

Maman's to my grandmother's. Everybody knows I can be a beast when pushed too far, including Misty.

"*You have to focus, Jayd and let Mama's powers do their thing,*" my mom says, from her mind to mine. Her words cool my emotions and allow Mama's vision to dominate my sight once again. I'm glad that I didn't have a chance to remove my bracelets.

"You should know that toys are for young kids, Misty. Act your age."

I catch Misty's reflection in the window and use the makeshift mirror to my advantage. Mama taught me well and it's going to take every talent in my arsenal to beat these bitches at their own games. My eyes begin to change from brown to green and light up the dim room.

Misty tries to avoid direct eye contact but it's no use. I force her to look straight ahead and catch her site in mine.

"Let them go." Misty succumbs to my will but not without exacting a bit of revenge of her own.

"Isn't it bad luck for daughters of Oshune to cut their hair without her permission?" Like the true hoodrat that she is, Misty grabs my ponytail and cuts it off with her claws.

"Damn it!" I shout as my ponytail falls from the back of my head. "You're going to pay for that." I focus all of my ancestors' combined powers on her and cause her to completely lose her shit.

"Jayd, stop it, please! I can't take anymore," she begs, but my sympathy for this trick has run out. Overpowered, Misty's limp body slithers down to the floor and my hair with her.

I can't worry about my impromptu trim right now. I have to protect Mama's soul before Esmeralda figures out what I've done to her favorite godchild. Another one of Esmeralda's birds is outside of the bedroom window taking notes for its master no doubt. Maybe I can use her pet to my advantage yet again. It's time to pay Mama's nemesis a visit now that mine is knocked out cold.

"Here birdie birdie," I say, snatching the bird's sight with ease. I can feel a soul inside but who does it belong to? It really doesn't matter because right now I need it to guard Mama who's still out of it. I'll worry about soul matching later.

I open the window and grab the bird before it can make a sound. "You will stay here and guard my grandmother." I feel the pet's obedience as I put it along with my grandmother in the closet for safekeeping. I would get Lexi but I'll be damned if she gets hurt again on my watch.

"Sorry about this, Mama, but I'll be back as soon as I can."

"You haven't seen evil yet."
-Esmeralda
Drama High, volume 9: Holidaze

~16~
SWEET DREAMS

With Misty knocked out on the floor and Mama in a spiritual coma, I had to call Netta in for support. Also, the window for dismantling Esmeralda is closing swiftly and I can't leave Mama alone with the enemy, even if she is temporarily on a mental lock down. The opportunity's too perfect and another one like this may not come around again. I have to take advantage of it tonight if I want it to be over.

"Where's your army or soldiers or whatever you called them when we told you that this was a bad idea?" Netta asks, not holding back any punches. She's wearing pajamas and rollers and is very pissed at me.

"I don't know. One minute they were outside arguing with Mickey and G, the next they were all nowhere to be found." I hope that Mickey was smart enough to go home.

"That doesn't sound good." Netta opens the closet door and carefully helps Mama into her bed. "Put the bird in that box, Jayd."

I grab the cardboard box she brought with her and gently place the bird inside. "It's in."

"Good. Now, since you're in such a rush to wear your grandmother's crown, go ahead and do whatever it is you had planned."

"Are you kidding? After Misty's sneak attack I'm not so sure about my plan. It seems like everything that I've tried lately is failing miserably."

"Suck it up, little girl," Netta says, taking my chin in her hand and shaking it roughly. "There's no time for doubt, Jayd. Your grandmother needs you and so do those silly boys you convinced to help you do the stupidest thing ever." Netta lets go of my tear stained face and softens her stance. "I know you're scared but remember what your Mama told you. Feed your faith to starve your fears. And right now, your fears need a bird."

"Okay, Netta. You're right," I say, wiping my eyes. "I started this mess. Now I have to clean it up." If I don't Mama's soul might be forever lost inside of whatever crazy dream Misty spun with that doll.

"I know, child. Now get to stepping," Netta says, turning her attention to her best friend.

"Wish me luck," I say, heading for the door.

"You cannot go to spiritual war in your street clothes, iyawo."

I sometimes forget that I'm a priestess in training. Remembering that I just did laundry this morning, I run outside to the spirit room where I keep all of my new clothes. I reach into the bag and grab the first dress that I see.

"I got it," I say, waving the multicolored sundress in the air as I make my way back toward the main house. It's the first dress I wore when I was allowed to wear colors again. The shopping spree before school began seems like a distant memory although it was less than two months ago. I miss Nellie and Mickey. I also miss Misty without fangs, claws, and all of her other evil attributes. Maybe getting psychically knocked the hell out will do her ass some good.

"Good, little Jayd," Netta says. "We need you to have as little outside influence on your head and body as possible. This is when the power of being an iyawo really comes in handy."

"I wish I could harness that power to help my friends keep it together. I never did hear back from Chase and it's not like him to ignore my calls. I'm really starting to get worried."

"Sometimes I wish you could have a simple high school life, Jayd, boyfriends and all," Netta says, stuffing several small fabric bags with various herbs, tobacco, and something else I can't quite put my finger on. "But it just wasn't meant to be for you. Your destiny is much greater than any of us can truly see and only the ancestors, the Orisha, and the Creator knows how it's all going to play out. It's my job to help you see your way through because it's a murky, dark, evil, twisted reality that we live in. And for everything it is, it is also its opposite. Use that to your advantage."

"Netta, I don't know what I would do without you. I can only hope that I'm half as good a godmother to Nickey as you are to me."

"Half the job of being a good godparent is being there for her and you are there, Jayd. Whatever you do, don't lose your connection with that baby. She's going to need you for the rest of her life, especially with the parents she's got to deal with. What the hell happened to your hair?" Netta asks, just noticing the alteration.

"Misty's revenge." I catch a glimpse of myself in the mirror above the shrine. After all the time I spent on my hair this past weekend I can't believe Misty cut it off. "I'm ready," I say, twirling what's left of my hair into a bun at the nape of my neck.

"So am I," Netta says, collecting all of the spiritual weaponry she's spent the last few minutes compiling. "Let's bring this bitch to her knees once and for all and show her who the real queen is around here."

"I couldn't agree more." With my voodoo dolls and mirrors in hand I follow Netta out of the house and onto the front porch.

225

"What about Mama, Misty, and the bird?"

"They'll be fine as long as you do your job," Netta says, taking me by the hand and courageously marching forward.

"Now, let's go kill ourselves a crow," Maman says, taking over my sight. "We will start with the eyes, just like with a voodoo doll. Go after what you want to control first."

We walk down the steps, across the driveway just like G did a moment ago, and up Esmeralda's front steps. Once we're inside the gated porch her animals go crazy, as usual.

"I'll stay outside and keep watch," Netta says, placing the stuffed bags across the threshold. "Here Jayd, you're going to need this." She reaches inside of her bag and pulls out the longest needle I've ever seen.

"That one, right there," Maman says, directing my eyes to Esmeralda's favorite crow in its cage. I recognize the bird's defeated soul.

"I don't know if I can do this," I think. I look at the poor animal and feel sympathy for the life I'm about to take. It unwillingly saved me from Esmeralda's venomous spider and now I have to sacrifice it to save Mama. What did any of her animals do to deserve this fate?

"Poor bird?" Maman says, shouting loudly into my thoughts. "That poor bird attacked my daughter, your grandmother, and I want its head on a platter for it!"

"Maman, this wasn't part of the plan," I say, but my great-grandmother could care less.

"We must move quickly, Jayd, before she makes more dolls out of you and my daughter. You must end this right now or you won't have another chance. Show her no mercy."

"But this isn't a doll," I say, as my jade eyes again take on a luminescent glow.

"Even better." Maman, with me at the helm, takes the long needle and kisses the tip before empowering me with the sharp tool.

I take the bird in my hands and quiet its cries. "I'm sorry." I raise my right hand ready to end the bird's suffering when its master, along with one of her followers, comes through the front door.

"I think you have someone that belongs to me, and I have a gift for you too, little girl," Esmeralda says. She unveils her hooded escort; it's Chase.

"What have you done to him?" I say, in utter disbelief. "If you hurt one hair on his head I will kill you and burn this house to the ground, Esmeralda. I swear it!" Without hesitation, or Maman's control, I pierce

227

the black bird in the eye and apparently Esmeralda's left eye along with it. Interesting.

"You'll pay for that!" she screams out in pain. "An eye for an eye, as they say."

Oh no. What have I done? Chase is completely overwhelmed by Esmeralda's sight. He looks like he wants to look at me but she's holding his will hostage.

"You really thought that some stupid little boys would be a match for me? You should've listened to your grandmother, Jayd. I was ready for you before you were even thought of, little girl."

"Put her to sleep now, Jayd. Put her to sleep!" Maman screams into my mind.

"And I was born ready for you." I remove the needle from the bird's eye and stab it trough the heart while focusing on Esmeralda's good eye.

"You little bitch!" Esmeralda lets go of Chase's mind who snaps out of whatever spell she put him under.

He's still too weak to speak but I can tell that he's fully aware of what's going on.

"I've got the boy," Netta says, opening the gate and signaling for Chase to follow her out. "Finish her, Jayd."

"It's Maman Marie in your head isn't it, little girl," Esmeralda says, panting like one of her dogs.

"Actually, yes it is," I say, walking up to her crumpled body on the ground. "She sends her love." I place the bird's carcass next to its owner and watch as Esmeralda slowly leaves this incarnation.

"You can tell Marie that I'll see her in hell, Jayd, and you too. Sooner than you think."

Every animal in Esmeralda's twisted menagerie howls as the crescent moon takes hold of the night sky. I would say that I'm sorry to see her go, but I'm not. I don't know if I'm ready to wear Mama's crown, but I'm damned sure not going to let anyone else steal it right off of her head. Esmeralda's reign as Mama's evil reflection is officially over. Now maybe we can have the peace that our lineage finally deserves.

EPILOGUE

The early morning sky gives way to the sunrise and ushers in a new day and all of the possibilities that come along with it. The air seems new and different this morning because it rained all night long. After a very chaotic dream last night everything seems to be back right and balanced, but never straight. As Mama said, life is as crooked as it gets.

I catch a glimpse of myself in the expensive looking wall mirror and notice that my eyes are back to normal. I had high hopes that like my mother's powers Maman's sight would also last. I guess that was sweet dreaming on my part.

Once Netta settled Mama into the spirit room with Misty and the bird in a deep sleep, I drove Chase home in Netta's truck. Chase and I slept together last night for the last time. I couldn't help but jump his bones after all that we went through. We made love on the balcony out in the rain, and it was beautiful.

I've decided that Chase and I can't be together and that's final. After all, I have to take his memories of what happened to him last night and bury them under the very same jade stones that he helped me find on the first night that we made love. I wish I could be with him but it's too dangerous. Because I love him, Esmeralda might try to find her way back through his dreams and I can't let that happen.

In the end, I love Chase and would never intentionally cause him pain, and I know that he feels the same way about me. Besides, our love affair is still our little secret and best friends should always keep each other's secrets, especially when they're shared.

Discussion Questions

1. Did Jayd have the right to slap Keenan for his comments about Nellie? Did he have a valid point?

2. Is there ever an acceptable scenario for a man to hit a woman or vice-versa? Explain.

3. In what way can Jayd and Rah ever be together, if at all?

4. Do you think that Jayd and Chase are meant to be together? Why or why not?

5. Do you know of any teenaged couples that live together? Do you think this is a good idea? Explain.

6. Should Mickey consider giving up her daughter to Nigel so that Nickey can have a better life with Nigel's family?

7. Who do you think Marcia really is?

8. Is Jayd's mom right to basically leave Jayd to fend for herself now that she's a senior in high school?

9. Should Jayd continue to work under Summer or not?

10. Do you think that Esmeralda's gone for good?

Stay tuned for the next book
in the DRAMA HIGH series,
ROGUE

RECOMMENDED READING

Listed below are a few of my favorite writers. The list is in no particular order and always changing. Please feel free to send me your favorites at **www.DramaHigh.com.**

Octavia E. Butler

Alice Walker

Zora Neale Hurston

Tina McElroy Ansa

James Baldwin

Maryse Conde

Madison Smart Bell

R.M. Johnson

Napoleon Hill

Jackie Collins

Mary Higgins Clark

J.K. Rowling

Stephen King

Iyanla Vanzant

Rhonda Byrne

Amy Tan

Nathan McCall

Nikki Giovanni

Edwidge Danticat

J. California Cooper

Toni Cade Bambara

Richard Wright

Gloria Naylor

James Patterson

Luisah Teish

Queen Afua

Bri. Maya Tiwari

Hill Harper

Joseph Campbell

Tananarive Due

Anne Rice

L.A. Banks

Francine Pascal

Sandra Cisneros

Danielle Steele

Carolyn Rodgers

Stephanie Rose Bird

Chief FAMA

Gwendolyn Brooks

Bell Hooks

Amiri Baraka

START YOUR OWN BOOK CLUB

Courtesy of the DRAMA HIGH series

ABOUT THIS GUIDE

The following is intended to help you get the Book Club you've always wanted up and running! Enjoy!

Start Your Own Book Club

A Book Club is not only a great way to make friends, but is also a fun and safe environment for you to express your views and opinions on everything from fashion to teen pregnancy? A Teen Book Club can also become a forum or venue to air grievances and plan remedies for problems.

The People
To start, all you need is yourself and at least one other person. There's no criteria for who this person or persons should be other than a desire to read and a commitment to read and discuss during a certain time frame.

The Rules
Just like in Jayd's life, sometimes even Book Club discussions can be filled with much drama. People tend to disagree with each other, cut each other off when speaking, and take criticism personally. So, there should be some ground rules:

1. Do not attack people for their ideas or opinions.
2. When you disagree with a book club member on a point, disagree respectfully. This means that you do not denigrate another person for their ideas or even their ideas, themselves i.e. no name calling or saying, "That's stupid!" Instead, say, "I can respect your position, however, I feel differently."
3. Back up your opinions with concrete evidence, either from the book in question or life in general.
4. Allow every one a turn to comment.
5. Do not cut a member off when they are speaking. Respectfully, wait your turn.
6. Critique only the idea (and do so responsibly; again, saying simply, "That's stupid!" is not allowed). Do not critique the person.
7. Every member must agree to and abide by the ground rules.

*Feel free to add any other ground rules you think might be necessary.

The Meeting Place

Once you've decided on members, and agreed to the ground rules, you should decide on a place to meet. This could be the local library, the school library, your favorite restaurant, a bookstore, or a member's home. Remember, though, if you decide to hold your sessions at a member's home, the location should rotate to another member's home for the next sessions. It's also polite for guests to bring treats when attending a Book Club meeting at a member's home. If you choose to hold your meetings in a public place, always remember to ask the permission of the librarian or store manager. If you decide to hold your meetings in a local bookstore, ask the manager to post a flyer in the window announcing the Book Club to attract more members if you so desire.

Timing is Everything

Teenagers of today are all much busier than teenagers of the past. You're probably thinking, "Between Chorus Rehearsals, the Drama Club, and oh yeah, my job, when will I ever have time to read another book that doesn't feature Romeo and Juliet!" Well, there's always time, if it's time well-planned and time planned ahead. You and your Book Club can decide to meet as often or as little as is appropriate for your bustling schedules. **Once a month** is a favorite option. **Sleepover Book Club** meetings—if you're open to excluding one gender—is also a favorite option. And in this day of high-tech, savvy teens, **Internet Discussion Groups** are also an appealing option. Just choose what's right for you!

Well, you've got the people, the ground rules, the place, and the time. All you need now is a book!

The Book

Choosing a book is the most fun. SWEET DREAMS is of course an excellent choice, and since it's a series, you won't soon run out of books to read and discuss. Your Book Club can also have comparative discussions as you compare the first book, THE FIGHT, to the second, SECOND CHANCE, and so on.

But depending on your reading appetite, you may want to veer outside of the DRAMA HIGH series. That's okay. There are plenty of options available.

Don't be afraid to mix it up. Nonfiction is just as good as fiction, and a fun way to learn about from whence we came without the monotony of a history book. Science Fiction and Fantasy can be fun too!

And always, always, research the author. You may find the author has a website where you can post your Book Club's questions or comments. The author may even have an email address available so you can correspond directly. Authors will also sit in on your Book Club, either in person, or on the phone, and this can be a fun way to discuss the boo as well!

The Discussion

Every good Book Club discussion starts with questions. **SWEET DREAMS,** as well as every other book in the **DRAMA HIGH** series comes along with a Reading Group Guide for your convenience, though of course, it's fine to make up your own. Here are some sample questions to get started:

1. What's this book all about anyway?
2. Who are the characters? Do we like them? Do they remind us of real people?
3. Was the story interesting? Were real issues of concern to you examined?
4. Were there details that didn't quite work for you or ring true?
5. Did the author create a believable environment—one that you can visualize?
6. Was the ending satisfying?
7. Would you read another book from this author?

Record Keeper

It's generally a good idea to have someone keep track of the books you read. Often libraries and schools will hold reading drives where you're rewarded for having read a certain number of books in a certain time period. Perhaps, a pizza party awaits!

Get Your Teachers and Parents Involved

Teachers and Parents love it when kids get together and read. So involve your teachers and parents. Your Book Club may read a particular book where it would help to have an adult's perspective as part of the discussion. Teachers may also be able to include what you're doing as a Book Club in the classroom curriculum. That way books you love to read like DRAMA HIGH can find a place in your classroom alongside of the books you don't love to read so much.

CPSIA information can be obtained
at www.ICGtesting.com
Printed in the USA
BVOW06s2151031216
469712BV00008B/105/P